WRITTEN BY AYUN HALLIDAY
ILLUSTRATED BY PAUL HOPPE

schwartz & wade books • new york

WRITER'S ACKNOWLEDGMENTS

Thanks to Rebecca Sherman, Anne Schwartz, and Paul Hoppe for conspiring to put this book in your hands, Mary Ellen Bontempo-Singer for providing character inspiration whilst serving as the World's Greatest School Nurse, Aeden Mlanao for reminding me to remain accountable to those with genuine peanut allergies, the staff of the late, great Gramstand for letting me spend upwards of six hours a day writing in their basement, Alex Cox for fueling my family's love of graphic novels, E. Lockhart for her ongoing good advice and encouragement, indie comic shops everywhere for bravely managing to exist at all, and all the lovely guerrilla marketeers who bring it on behalf of *The East Village Inky*.

A great big howdy-do to those who remember me from high school, both friends and former adversaries (some of whom I now claim as friends, thanks to the miracle of Facebook . . . which, like cell phones and for the most part peanut allergies, didn't exist back then).

As ever, my biggest thanks are reserved for Greg, India, Milo, and to a lesser degree, Mungo Kotis.

Dare to Be Heinie. —A.H.

ILLUSTRATOR'S ACKNOWLEDGMENTS

Thanks to Ayun for letting me lend my visuals to her wonderful story, and to Rebecca, Anne, Lee, and Rachael for making this all possible. It's been a long ride; I couldn't have done it without all your help, input, and patience.

Thanks also to my friends and colleagues for always being there with encouragement and enthusiasm, especially to Anuj for all those after-work sessions. A special thank-you to Lauren for opening my eyes to the publishing world.

Most importantly, I want to thank my parents for their love and support, without which I would not be where I am today. —P.H.

TO INDIA, MILO, AND ANYONE WHO'S EVER SOUGHT TO STAND OUT IN A CROWD —A.H.

FOR MY FELLOW CARTOONISTS OUT THERE, WHO INSPIRE ME TO DRAW —P.H.

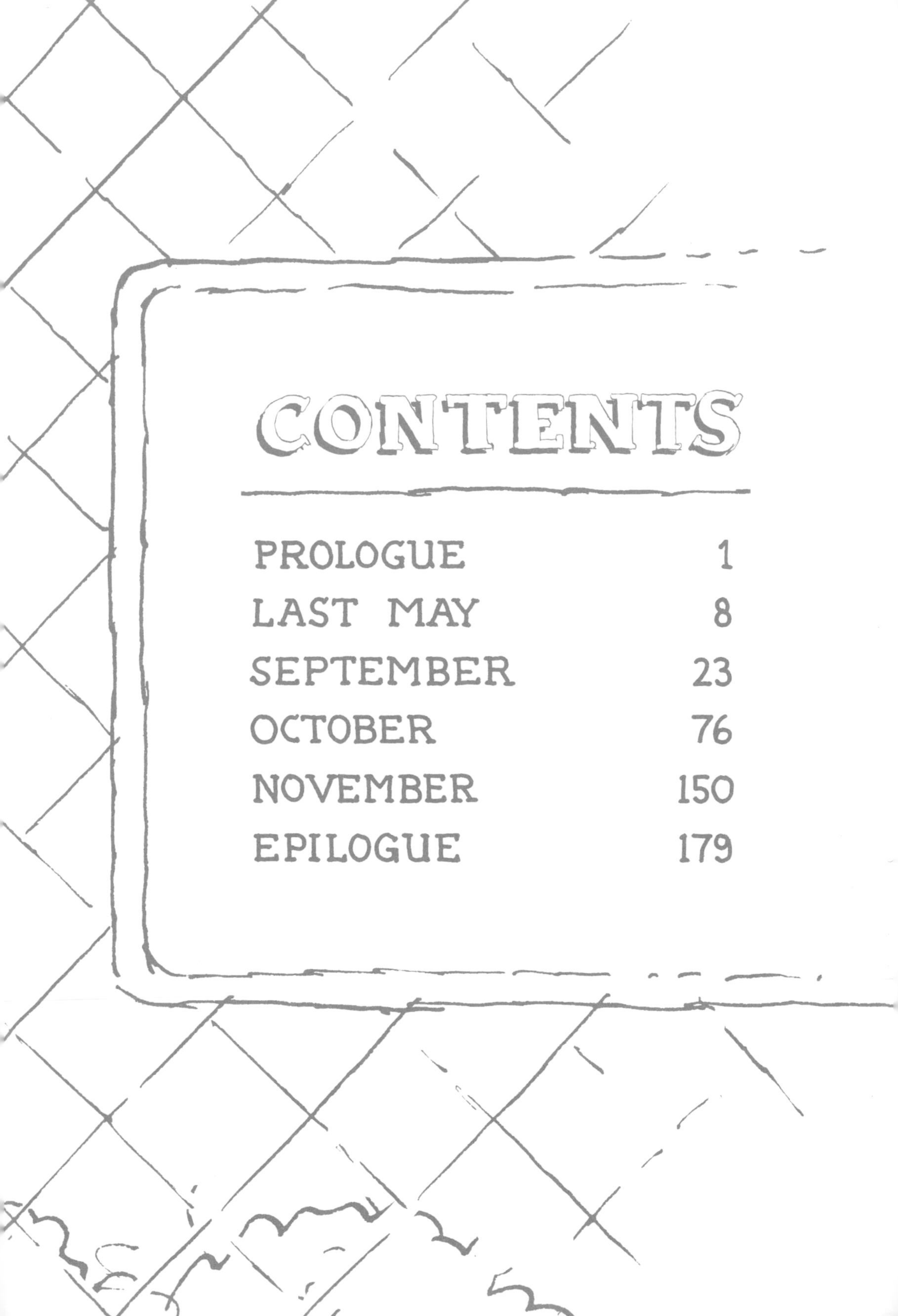

CONTENTS

PROLOGUE

NO ONE AT MY OLD SCHOOL KNEW ABOUT
MY PEANUT ALLERGY. . . .

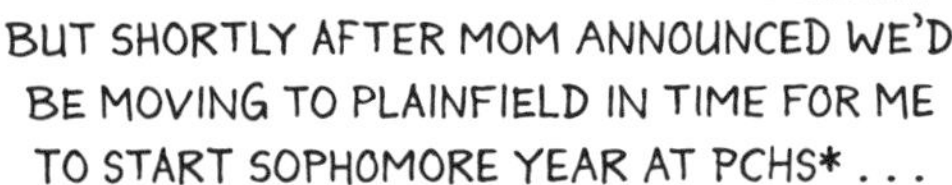

(*PCHS=PLAINFIELD COMMUNITY HIGH SCHOOL)

TO THEM, PEANUT BUTTER IS THIS INNOCUOUS THING THEY'VE MINDLESSLY SNARFED SINCE THEY WERE LIKE TWO.
POP!

TO ME, IT'S A KILLER—
ONE TASTE AND **BANG!** I'M DEAD.

ZOO GOT THAT RIGHT AWAY.
JUST THE TEENSIEST, BABY-FINGERNAIL-SIZED SCOOPFUL . . . LET'S NOT EVEN DISCUSS THAT THING I READ ON THE INTERNET, THAT GIRL WHO KISSED HER BOYFRIEND 15 MINUTES AFTER HE ATE A PEANUT BUTTER SANDWICH, WENT INTO SHOCK, AND DIED.
I'D KILL MYSELF BEFORE I'D LET ANYTHING LIKE THAT HAPPEN TO US.
ZOO'S THE BEST.

TOO BAD NOT EVERYONE'S AS PERCEPTIVE AS HE IS.
I'M LIKE, "COULD YOU STOP TALKING ABOUT YOUR STUPID PEANUT ALLERGY EVERY FIVE SECONDS?"
I'M SORRY BUT I DON'T CARE!
FOR REAL! I'M LIKE, "OH MY GOD, STOP ACTING LIKE YOU'VE GOT CANCER!"
NICE, HUH?
OH YEAH. I ALMOST FORGOT. I DID HAVE ONE OTHER LITTLE PROBLEM, BESIDES THOSE GUYS. SEE, THE THING IS . . .
I'M NOT REALLY ALLERGIC TO PEANUTS.

LAST MAY
COMBO-MEAL 1
EXCUSE ME . . .

CAN YOU TELL ME WHERE YOU GOT YOUR ID BRACELET? THAT CLUNKY CHAIN LOOKS WICKED COOL.
ARE YOU HIGH?
NO OFFENSE, OKAY? I'D GIVE IT TO YOU FOR KEEPS,
BUT I'M NOT ALLOWED TO TAKE IT OFF.
WHY?
WELL, YA NEVER KNOW WHEN YOU'RE GONNA KEEL OVER FROM ANAPHYLACTIC SHOCK.
LIKE FOR EPILEPSY AND DIABETES?
"IT'S A MEDICAL ALERT BRACELET."
SEVERE ALLERGY TO PEANUTS CARLA
YEP, BUT IN MY CASE, IT'S BECAUSE I'M ALLERGIC TO PEANUTS.

OH . . . FORGIVE ME FOR BEING DENSE, BUT IF YOU KNOW YOU'RE ALLERGIC, CAN'T YOU JUST NOT EAT THEM?
COMBO-MEAL!

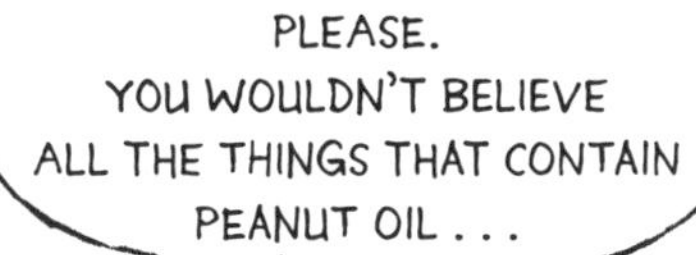
PLEASE. YOU WOULDN'T BELIEVE ALL THE THINGS THAT CONTAIN PEANUT OIL . . .

. . . OR WERE PROCESSED IN A PLACE THAT ALSO PROCESSES PEANUTS . . .

LIKE, MY FRIENDS ALL LOVE THAI FOOD, RIGHT? BUT WHENEVER WE GO TO A THAI RESTAURANT, THERE'S NOTHING FOR ME TO EAT!
EVERYTHING'S GOT PEANUTS!
BUT IF YOU TELL THE RESTAURANT YOU'RE ALLERGIC—

YOU MEAN ASK THEM TO HOLD THE PEANUTS?
HEY, GREEEEEAT IDEA!

EXCEPT WHAT IF THE WAITRESS DOESN'T SPEAK ENGLISH?
OR THE CHEF'S ONE OF THOSE A-HOLES WHO'S CONVINCED ONLY FINICKY JERKS MAKE SPECIAL REQUESTS?
HOLD THE PEANUTS! HOLD THE PEANUTS!!! HOW 'BOUT I GRIND 'EM UP SO FINE YOU CAN'T NOTICE?!
ONE PEANUT-Y SPECK AND MY FACE PUFFS UP,
MY THROAT SWELLS SHUT—
THAT SUCKS.
MY MOM WON'T LET ME OUT OF THE HOUSE WITHOUT MY EPIPEN—
WHAT'S THAT?
THIS SYRINGE-Y THING I JAB MYSELF WITH IF I SUSPECT I ACCIDENTALLY INGESTED SOME PEANUTS. I'VE ONLY USED IT TWICE.
DID IT WORK?
WELL, OBVIOUSLY. I'M HERE, AREN'T I?

I'M NOT ENTIRELY SURE HOW, BUT IT'S GOT THIS STUFF THAT JUST, LIKE, STOPS THE ALLERGIC REACTION COLD.
SOUNDS LIKE A GOOD THING TO HAVE.
I GUESS, BUT IT'S LIKE, ALL THIS DRAMA, YOU KNOW?
IF A DISH SEEMS RISKY, I TEND TO STEER CLEAR.
OH, CARLA, YOU'RE TOO YOUNG TO DIE!
SHUT UP, STEPHANIE.
MAY I TAKE YOUR ORDER, PLEASE?
NICE TALKING TO YOU.

SNACK WRAPS
CAN YOU TELL ME WHAT'S IN THE RODEO SAUCE?
?
NO
CHOKING VICTIM

LATER THAT NIGHT
MEDICAL ALERT BRACELETS
YOUR INFORMATION
NAME: SADIE WILDHACK
ADDRESS: 182 WI
WRIST SIZE:
PEANUT ALLERGY
I'M NOT EXACTLY SURE WHAT GOT INTO ME . . .

MAYBE IT WAS THIS CHAT WITH MY FRIEND CHERYL . . .
IS HOTTIE MCSIXPACK GOING WITH YOU TO PCHS?
NO, YOU CAN HAVE HIM.
I NEVER THOUGHT I'D LIVE TO SEE THE DAY.
WEREN'T YOU GOING TO GET HIS NAME TATTOOED ON YOUR BUTT?
PLEASE. HE'S PROBABLY GAY.
I WISH YOU WEREN'T LEAVING.
ME TOO.

ACTUALLY, I WISH I COULD TRADE PLACES.
IT'S LIKE YOU GET A DO-OVER. MAYBE YOU'LL EVEN BE POPULAR!
DREAM ON.
OKAY, BUT YOU KNOW WHAT I MEAN.
SOME OF US GET TO SPEND THE NEXT THREE YEARS AS THE DELUDED FATTY WHOSE PANTS SPLIT DURING CHEERLEADER TRYOUTS. . . .
MATH
CHERYL, I KNOW THAT WAS A HUGE DEAL AS FAR AS YOU'RE CONCERNED, BUT SWEAR TO GOD, PEOPLE DO HAVE OTHER THINGS TO THINK ABOUT.
SURE THEY DO, UNTIL I COME INTO THE ROOM, AND THEN THEY'RE LIKE, "OH MY GOD, THERE SHE IS!"

IF IT WERE ME, I'D TEAR EVERYTHING OUT.
?
YOU KNOW HOW YOU'RE SUPPOSED TO BEFORE YOU PLANT A NEW GARDEN? I'D LET EVERYONE THINK I WAS AN EXCHANGE STUDENT FROM PERU.
I'D BE LIKE, "EEN PERU, WE DRINK WINE IN ZE CAFETERIA AND RECOGNIZE CHEERLEADING FOR ZE BARBARIC ACTIVITY EET EES."
THAT'D WIN 'EM OVER.
YOU SCOFF, BUT EVERYONE ELSE WOULD BE LIKE, "OOH, THAT NEW GIRL'S SO SOPHISTICATED!"
BETTER WORK ON YOUR PERUVIAN ACCENT.
PFFF! LIKE ANYONE IN PLAINFIELD WOULD DARE CHALLENGE ME.

DO YOU EVEN KNOW WHAT THE CAPITAL OF PERU IS?
POLITICS
I'D FIND THAT OUT, IF I WERE YOU.
OR I COULD JUST MAKE SOMETHING UP!
IT'S LIMA, RIGHT?
BEATS ME!
YOU'RE HOPELESS.
WELL, I GUESS THAT'S IT.
YUP.

YOU WANT ONE LAST SMOOCH?
HE'S ALL YOURS NOW.
DON'T WORRY, TRAVIS. I'LL BE GENTLE.
HAVE YOU CONSIDERED CONSULTING A DOCTOR?
FOR WHAT? BIRTH CONTROL?
FOR YOUR MENTAL DISEASE.

YEAH, WELL, ANYWAY . . .
SADIE! ARE YOU EXPECTING A PACKAGE?
WHO'S MS INDUSTRIES?
KLONK
KLONK
MUST BE THIS COMPANY I ORDERED EARRINGS FROM. I WANTED TO GIVE CHERYL SOMETHING TO REMEMBER ME BY.
FOR PETE'S SAKE, SADIE, PLAINFIELD'S BARELY AN HOUR'S DRIVE! YOU'LL SEE EACH OTHER AGAIN.

I KNOW, BUT—
YIPES, THAT REMINDS ME! IF I DON'T FILL OUT THAT CARD OUR MAIL WON'T GET FORWARDED. . . .
RRIP

SEVERE ALLERGY
TO PEANUTS
SADIE WILDHACK

SEPTEMBER
BEFORE YOU WRITE ME OFF AS SOME KIND OF MESSED-UP DELUSIONAL PSYCHO . . .
WELCOME BACK, PCHS
. . . THINK ABOUT WHAT IT'S LIKE TO BE THROWN INTO A SITUATION WHERE EVERYONE KNOWS EVERYONE . . . AND NO ONE KNOWS YOU.

YOU LOOK REALLY CUTE.
I MEAN COOL.
MOM!
THIS TIME TOMORROW, YOU'LL HAVE NEW FRIENDS COMING OUT YOUR EARS.
GENUINE EXCHANGE STUDENT FROM BOLIVIA*
*WHICH COINCIDENTALLY BORDERS PERU.
DON'T OPEN YOUR MOUTH.
LET THEM THINK YOU'RE AN AMERICAN.

EXCUSE ME, I'M LOOKING FOR 603A. IT WAS SUPPOSED TO BE NEXT TO THE LIBRARY BUT IT'S NOT.
URM . . . YES . . . URM, ESPAÑOL?
WHAT?
URM, YOU SPEAK ESPAÑOL?
OH SORRY! I . . . UH, NO.
I SORRY.
SORRY.
DON'T WORRY. IT'S OKAY.
GOOD LUCK!

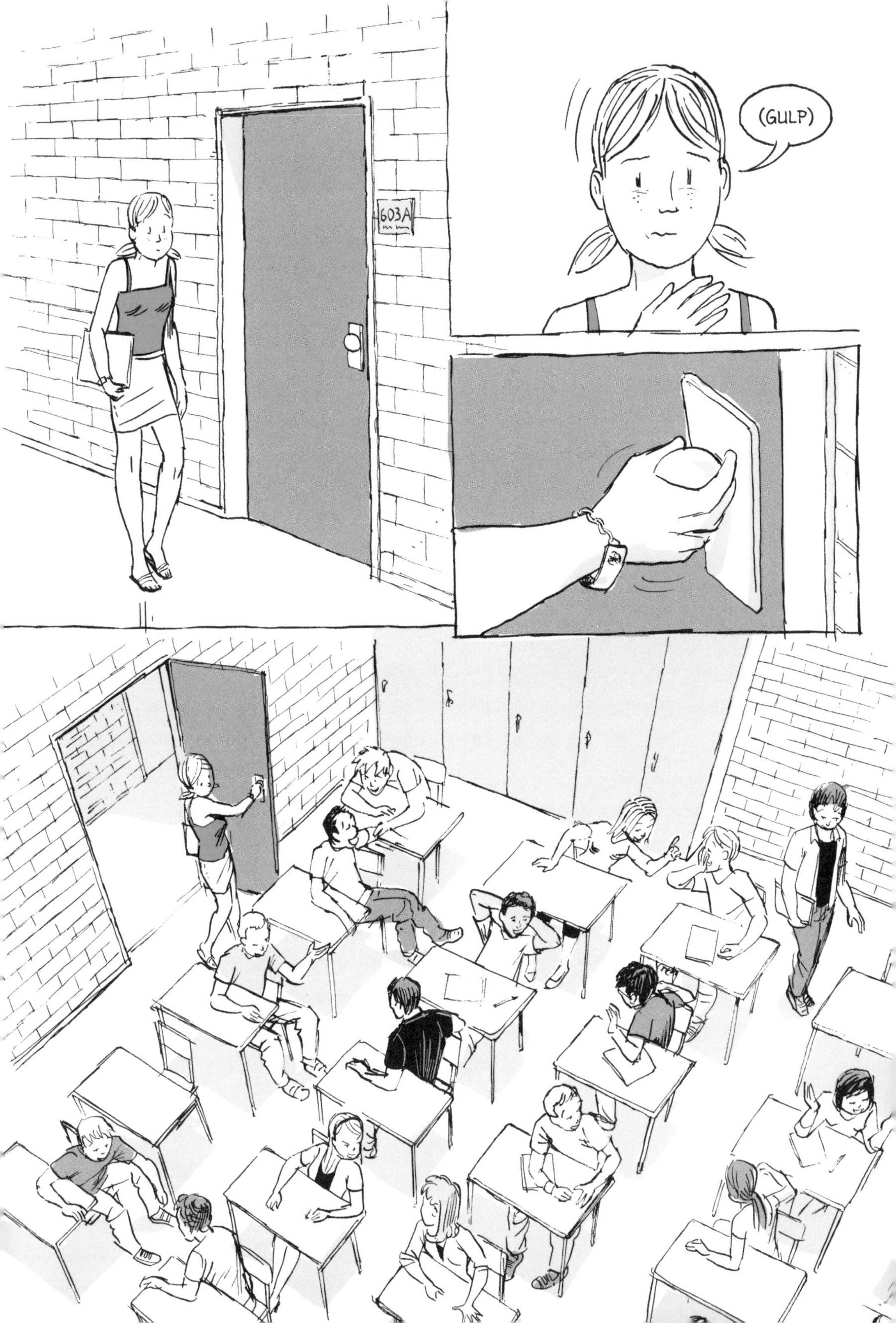
603A
(GULP)

OH MY GOD, DID YOU CHECK OUT PAUL C?
I KNOW, IT'S LIKE, WHAT HAPPENED? HE USED TO BE SUCH A LITTLE GEEK!
NOT ANYMORE!
WHAT ABOUT LISA P?
PLEASE! HUMAN SKELETON IS NOT AN ATTRACTIVE LOOK.
DERRICK SAID HE SAW HER IN A BIKINI AT THE POOL AND ALMOST THREW UP.
SWEET! LISA P'S ANOREXIA GAVE DERRICK BULIMIA!
GIRL, YOU ARE SICK.
HI.
UM . . . I LIKE YOUR SHOES.

OH . . . THANKS.
I'M SADIE.
CELIA.
LESLIE.
HI.
HI.
SO, CAN YOU EVEN BELIEVE ABOUT MCCLOSKEY'S WIFE DUMPING HIM FOR HER YOGA INSTRUCTOR?
HER *FEMALE* YOGA INSTRUCTOR!
HE DESERVES IT FOR MAKING US CUT UP ALL THOSE INNOCENT FROGS!

OKAY, PIPE DOWN! PIPE DOWN!
TEENAGE HORMONES . . .
YOU'LL HAVE AN ENTIRE SCHOOL YEAR TO FIND OUT ABOUT EACH OTHER'S SUMMER VACATIONS.
SHUT IT!!!

THAT'S BETTER.
NOW, MANY OF YOU ALREADY HAVE THE MISFORTUNE TO KNOW ME.
AND THOSE WHO DON'T WILL SOON ENOUGH.
BEYOND INITIATING YOU INTO THE MYSTERIES OF ALGEBRA,
I AM, AS YOUR HOMEROOM TEACHER, THE ONE TO WHOM YOU'LL COME WHEN YOU HAVE A PROBLEM.
MR. LARCH

IF MS. WILSON THROWS YOU TO THE GROUND AND STEALS YOUR BUS PASS, SEE ME.
IF MR. SUZUKI MAKES UNWANTED SUGGESTIONS OR ADVANCES OF A SEXUAL NATURE, SEE ME.
DO NOT SEE ME IF YOU ARE UNPREPARED FOR A TEST OR YOUR HOMEWORK IS OVERDUE. UNLESS YOU'RE EXPIRING FROM SOME TRAGIC TEENAGE DISEASE, I DO NOT WANT TO HEAR IT!
NOW, MAY I HAVE AN ABLE-BODIED VOLUNTEER TO ASSIST IN THE DISTRIBUTION OF OUR SACRED TEXT?
ALGEBRA

(*I WOULD LIKE TO MAKE VOMIT NOW.)

UGH. HE'S SO QUEER.
SO'S MR. LARCH.
THE TWO OF THEM SHOULD GO OUT.
OH MY GOD, WAIT! MELANIE MARCO'S PURSE? I'M LIKE, "WHAT ARE YOU, TEN YEARS OLD?"
TRY SEVEN.
SHUT UP!
OH MY GOD!!!!!!
SHE'S TOTALLY CHOKING ME!
DO YOU LIKE HOW SAMMI FRIEDMAN'S PANTS MAKE IT LOOK LIKE SHE'S POPPING A BONER?
PLEASE. WITH A MUSTACHE LIKE THAT, SHE PROBABLY IS.

EXCUSE ME, CAN YOU TELL ME IF THIS HAS PEANUTS IN IT?
WHAT'D YOU SAY, BABY DOLL?
I NEED TO KNOW IF THERE ARE ANY PEANUTS IN HERE.
IN THE TURKEY ROLL?
I KNOW IT SOUNDS WEIRD, BUT I'M HIGHLY ALLERGIC.
DEXTER! YOU KNOW IF THE TURKEY ROLL HAS PEANUT IN IT?
OR PEANUT OIL, EITHER.
PEANUT? WHAT YOU MEAN PEANUT?
THIS ONE'S GOT ALLERGIES, CAN'T HAVE NO PEANUT.

I DON'T KNOW. YOU BETTER ASK REESEY.
REESEY!!!
NEVER MIND, THANKS.
I THINK I'LL JUST GO WITH A YOGURT OR SOMETHING.
OKAY, *THAT* WAS EMBARRASSING.

I'M LIKE, "IN YOUR DREAMS, BOY!"
WET DREAMS, MAYBE.
OKAY, OBVIOUSLY THESE GIRLS AND I ARE NOT IN THE SAME LEAGUE.
PARTLY BECAUSE EITHER ONE OF THEM COULD HAVE STEPPED STRAIGHT OUT OF *TEEN VOGUE*.
TEEN VOGUE
TEEN VOGUE
AND PARTLY BECAUSE I'M NOT A TOTAL BITCH.
BUT YOU HAVE TO SIT WITH SOMEONE, RIGHT?
I MEAN, AT LEAST I'D TALKED TO THEM BEFORE.

YOU GUYS MIND IF I SIT HERE?
SURE, GO AHEAD.
I THINK WE'RE IN THE SAME HOMEROOM. SADIE.
OH YEAH. CELIA.
LESLIE.

GREETINGS, FELLOW YOGURT EATERS.
PLEASE TELL ME YOU DIDN'T NOTICE THAT SCENE BACK THERE. OH GOD, IT WAS SO MORTIFYING.
WHAT SCENE?
WITH THE PEANUTS. I WAS LIKE, "OH GOD, MAKE HER STOP!"
MAKE WHO STOP?

THE CAFETERIA LADY. I'VE GOT A SERIOUS PEANUT ALLERGY, SO BEFORE I EAT ANYTHING, I ALWAYS HAVE TO FIND OUT IF IT HAS PEANUTS IN IT—
YOGURT HAS PEANUTS IN IT?
NO, I WAS ASKING HER ABOUT THAT TURKEY ROLL THING.
ALL THE CAFETERIA WORKERS AT MY OLD SCHOOL KNEW MY DEAL. IF I WAS ABOUT TO EAT SOMETHING I SHOULDN'T, THEY'D GO,
UH-UH, BABY, THAT ONE'S SUICIDE.
BUT NOBODY HERE KNOWS ME YET. . . .
ANYWAY, I THOUGHT I'D DIE, THE WAY SHE STARTED SCREAMING HER HEAD OFF LIKE THAT.
OH . . . I DIDN'T NOTICE.
YAWN
I'M SORRY, BUT THAT TURKEY ROLL LOOKS LIKE A FETAL PIG DISSECTION.
CELIA!!!

YOU HOOKERS GONNA MOVE YOUR TRAYS SO I CAN SIT DOWN?
NITA!
OH MY GOD, I LOVE YOUR NEW HAIR!
OH YEAH. NITA, THIS IS SALLY.
SADIE.
GOD, CELIA!

SNAP__SNAP
AND THIS IS MAMACITA JUANITA CHIQUITA TACO-BELLITA!
AY, CHIHUAHUA!!
DAG, Y'ALL SOUND LIKE YOU'RE IN *WEST SIDE STORY*.
I FEEL PRETTY! OH SO PRETTY!
PLEASED TO MEET—
OH MY GOD! RUSTY!
RUST!!! OVER HERE!
OH HELL NO, LOOK AT HIS ARM!

OOH, IT ISN'T RUBBING OFF!
DID IT HURT?
HEY! WHO CAN WE GET TO BUY US SOME KAHLÚA?
OOH, WHITE RUSSIANS, YUMMY!
YOW, NITA! WAY TO GIVE ME AN INDIAN BURN!
IF WE ASK DALLAS, WE CAN USE HIS BROTHER'S ID!
DALLAS?
WHAT'S WRONG WITH DALLAS?
WE WOULDN'T HAVE TO, LIKE, TALK TO HIM.
FINE. ASK HIM.
YAY! WHITE RUSSIANS!

LATER THAT AFTERNOON
SO? HOW WAS IT?
GOOD, I GUESS.
"GOOD, I GUESS"?
SURELY YOU CAN DO BETTER THAN THAT.
CAN'T IT WAIT? I'VE GOT A TON OF HOMEWORK.
ON THE FIRST DAY? SHEESH!

ACTUALLY, THE ONLY TEACHER TO GIVE HOMEWORK THAT FIRST DAY WAS MR. LARCH.
MAN, I THOUGHT YOU SAID THIS WAS ALGEBRA!
IT'S ALSO YOUR HOMEROOM . . .
. . . AND THE PRINCIPAL'S WISH IS THAT EVERY STUDENT WILL INTRODUCE HIM- OR HERSELF TO HIS OR HER HOMEROOM TEACHER IN A ONE-PAGE, FIRST-PERSON ESSAY.
NOW, NOW, THIS TASK NEED NOT BE TORTURE.
JUST PRETEND YOU'RE TALKING TO A GOOD FRIEND.
WOULDN'T A FRIEND, LIKE, ALREADY KNOW THAT STUFF?
HEY, CHERYL, IT'S ME.
I WAS JUST WONDERING HOW THE FIRST DAY OF SCHOOL WENT.

MINE WAS OKAY, I GUESS.
I DIDN'T EXACTLY FIND MY PEEPS, BUT IT'S ONLY THE FIRST DAY, RIGHT?
ANYWAY, CALL ME. I CAN'T BELIEVE WE HAVEN'T TALKED SINCE YOU WENT TO CAMP.
DID IT SUCK?
I'M JUST KIDDING. I'M SURE IT WAS TOTALLY AWESOME.
OKAY, SO . . .
CALL ME. BYE.

NEW DOCUMENT
One of the most important things to know about me is_
TAK TAK TAK

I'M ALLERGIC TO PEANUTS.
TAK TAK

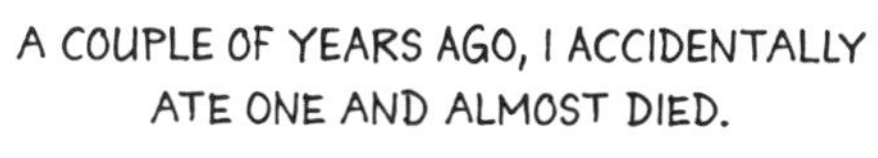
A COUPLE OF YEARS AGO, I ACCIDENTALLY ATE ONE AND ALMOST DIED.

KNOCK KNOCK

THE DOCTOR SAID HE'S NEVER SEEN AN ALLERGY AS STRONG AS MINE.
I THOUGHT YOU MIGHT LIKE A LITTLE SNACK.
TAK TAK
THANKS.

IT'S TOTALLY UNFAIR BUT THAT DOESN'T CHANGE THE FACTS.

THE SERIOUSNESS OF MY CONDITION INFLUENCES EVERYTHING I DO,

MOSTLY BY LIMITING WHAT I CAN DO.
MAYBE SOMEDAY THEY'LL FIND A CURE . . .
PEANU
TER
UNTIL THEN, I'LL LIVE LIFE TO THE FULLEST . . . AWARE THAT ANY MOMENT COULD BE MY LAST.
THANK YOU, MS. WILDHACK. YOU MAY SIT. MS. WILSON?
I'M SO SURE HE DIDN'T SAY WE'D BE READING THESE THINGS OUT LOUD.

SO WHAT WAS IT YOU ATE, THE TIME YOU NEARLY DIED?
MMMFPPH.
IT WAS A SUNDAE.
A SUNDAE!
YOU KNOW THOSE MONKEYBUSTER PARFAITS AT DAIRYLAND?
OH MAN!
DID YOU THINK IT WAS BANANAS ONLY?
NO. I WAS OUT WITH THIS FRIEND AND SHE WAS BUGGING ME FOR A BITE OF MY CONE.
AND I WAS LIKE, "UH-UH." BUT SHE'S LIKE, "PLEASE?"

AND I'M LIKE, "NO WAY." BUT SHE'S LIKE, "PLEASE-PLEASE-PRETTY-PLEASE."
WITH SUGAR ON TOP?
I'M LIKE,
CHERYL, C'MON, YOU'VE GOT YOUR OWN!
I KNOW, BUT PLEASE? I'LL TRADE YOU A BITE OF MINE!
IT'S WEIRD. IT'S LIKE THE WHOLE ALLERGY THING JUST FLEW OUT OF MY HEAD.
YOU ARE SUCH A BRAT.
THE LAST THING I REMEMBER WAS MY FRIEND SCREAMING
OH MY GOD! SOMEBODY CALL 911!
WOW. THAT MUST'VE BEEN TOTALLY INTENSE.
LUCKY FOR ME, CHERYL CALLED FOR HELP RIGHT AWAY.
AND THAT YOU HAD YOUR BRACELET.

EXCEPT I DIDN'T.
I'D LOST IT SWIMMING.
OH MY GOD.
BUT CHERYL WAS AWESOME.
SHE FILLED THE AMBULANCE GUY IN,
CALLED MY MOM . . .
THAT'S THE KIND OF FRIEND TO HAVE.
FOR REAL.
WIPIES
SHOULD'VE GIVEN HER A BITE
THE FIRST TIME SHE ASKED.
NO KIDDING!
BUT I DON'T GET HOW YOU COULD JUST,
LIKE, FORGET ABOUT SOMETHING
SO IMPORTANT.
WHAT CAN I SAY? IT HAPPENED.
I'M NOT SAYING IT
DIDN'T, IT'S JUST—

GOD, ANGELA, LIKE YOU'VE NEVER SPACED OUT ON ANYTHING THAT MATTERED.
YEAH, WHY DON'T YOU TELL SADIE ABOUT THE TIME YOU ACCIDENTALLY LEFT TIMMY AT THE MALL?
TIMMY?
HER FIVE-YEAR-OLD BROTHER.
OKAY, BUT CAN I JUST SAY? IF TIMMY WAS *YOUR* LITTLE BROTHER?
THAT SATAN'S SPAWN? PERISH THE THOUGHT!
WAIT, CAN WE BACK IT UP FOR A SEC? BECAUSE THE BELL'S GOING TO RING AND YOU NEVER FINISHED TELLING US ABOUT MR. MCCLOSKEY'S WIFE.
I'M SORRY, BUT THAT HAS GOT TO BE AN URBAN LEGEND.

TWO DAYS IN, AND ALREADY OPERATION PEANUT HAD REELED IN A COUPLE OF POTENTIAL FRIENDS. NOT BAD.
SEE YOU TOMORROW, SADIE!
I'LL SEND YOU THAT LINK I WAS TELLING YOU ABOUT.
CHERYL, CHERYL, BO BERREL, BANANA FANNA FOE FARRELL . . .
IT'S YOUR LONG-LOST FRIEND FROM PLAINFIELD COMMUNITY HIGH!
SO . . . YEAH . . . CALL ME!

OH. HI.
HEY.
YOU'VE GOT LARCH FOR HOMEROOM, RIGHT?
YEP.
ME TOO.
I KNOW.

YOURS WAS REALLY GOOD, TOO.
YOU THINK?
YEAH. THAT PART ABOUT THE . . . UM . . .
COMPUTERS?
YEAH! AND CELL PHONES, RIGHT! MY MOM GOES BERSERK WHEN I TEXT. IT COSTS EXTRA UNDER OUR PLAN—
YOU DID GET THAT I WAS BEING IRONIC, RIGHT?
OH YEAH, ABSOLUTELY—
I DON'T *REALLY* BELIEVE TEXT MESSAGES AND EMAIL ARE THE MOST UNCORRUPTED FORMS OF EXPRESSION.
OH . . . HA HA!
PURE UNADULTERATED EVIL, MAYBE . . .
?

LOOK, THE WAY I SEE IT, MODERN COMMUNICATIONS DO NOTHING BUT WREAK HAVOC ON THE BEAUTY OF HUMAN INTERACTION.
I REFUSE TO BE A PARTY TO IT. I DON'T HAVE A CELL PHONE. DON'T HAVE A COMPUTER.
YOU'RE KIDDING.
DON'T HAVE 'EM. DON'T WANT 'EM.
BUT WHAT ABOUT YOUR FRIENDS?
WHAT ABOUT 'EM?
ISN'T IT HARD TO STAY IN CONTACT?
I MANAGE.

AM I FREAKING YOU OUT?
NO. IT'S JUST . . . HOW DO YOU DO HOMEWORK?
SAME WAY I'VE BEEN DOING IT SINCE KINDERGARTEN. PENCIL. NOTEBOOK. THIS CRAZY PLACE CALLED THE LIBRARY.
WELL, ANYWAY. NICE WORK ON THE ESSAY.
WHAT'S YOUR NAME AGAIN?
SADIE.
I'M ZOO.

IT WASN'T LONG BEFORE I FOUND OUT HOW ZOO MANAGED . . .
WITHOUT EMAIL OR A CELL PHONE.
KNOCK KNOCK!

Mr. C. Suzuki requests the pleasure
of Ms. Wildhack's company.
Time: 12.15 pm
Date: Tomorrow
Place: The cafeteria
Luncheon to be provided
100% Peanut free

OKAY, MISSY, I AM GIVING YOU ONE MORE CHANCE TO CALL ME BACK AND THEN I'M GOING TO, I DON'T KNOW WHAT . . .
. . . CALL MR. MUNTZ AND TELL HIM WHAT YOU SAID ABOUT HIS BEARD. REMEMBER?
SERIOUSLY, THOUGH, CALL ME, OKAY?
BECAUSE OTHERWISE, I'M GONNA THINK YOU EITHER HATE ME . . .
. . . OR ELSE YOU'VE DUMPED ALL YOUR FRIENDS TO BE WITH YOUR HOT NEW BOYFRIEND, IN WHICH CASE . . .
. . . I WANNA KNOW ALL THE DETAILS, SO CALL ME! GOODBYE!

NEXT DAY
SADIE! WANNA SIT?
I ALREADY PROMISED TO EAT WITH THIS GUY FROM HOMEROOM.
WOO WOO!

YOU GOT MY NOTE.
YEAH. IT WAS NEAT THE WAY YOU HAD IT FOLDED.
I WASN'T SURE I HAD THE RIGHT HOUSE.
HOW DID YOU . . . ?
DIRECTORY ASSISTANCE.
I THOUGHT YOU DIDN'T HAVE A PHONE.
PERSONALLY, NO, BUT MY PARENTS DO.

SO BON APPÉTIT. I'VE GOT EGG SALAD IN MY BAG, TOO, IN CASE YOU DON'T EAT MEAT.
I EAT MEAT.
ME TOO. I DIDN'T IN SEVENTH AND EIGHTH GRADE.
NOW I'D SAY I'M LIKE 80% VEGETARIAN.

THIS SANDWICH IS REALLY GOOD.
SO, BESIDES THE PEANUT ALLERGY, WHAT IS THERE TO KNOW ABOUT SADIE WILDHACK?
I'M GLAD YOU'RE ENJOYING IT.
UM, WELL, LET'S SEE. MY PARENTS SPLIT UP WHEN I WAS THREE. I LIVE WITH MY MOM. SHE WRITES CATALOG DESCRIPTIONS FOR THIS SWEDISH BABY CLOTHING COMPANY.
KFFT!
HMM. FASCINATING.
I KNOW, ISN'T IT?
I'VE LIVED IN SIX-SEVEN-EIGHT HOUSES SINCE I WAS BORN.
YOU LIVED IN PINEHURST, RIGHT?
CEDARWOOD.
SORRY. I ALWAYS GET THOSE TWO CONFUSED.
PEK!

THERE'S PROBABLY NOT MUCH DIFFERENCE.
CEDARWOOD'S THE ONE WITH THE LLAMA SANCTUARY, RIGHT?
LLAMA SANCTUARY?
MUST BE PINEHURST.
NO, IT COULD BE CEDARWOOD. WE ONLY LIVED THERE LIKE THREE YEARS.
CRUNCH
I DON'T KNOW. THAT LLAMA SANCTUARY'S PRETTY HARD TO MISS.
THEY'VE GOT BILLBOARDS AND ALL.
BRING THE KIDS TO FEED THE LLAMAS!
VISIT THE LLAMA SHOP FOR A PAIR OF OUR WORLD-FAMOUS LLAMA'S-WOOL MITTENS!
STOP BY THE REFRESHMENT STAND FOR A DELICIOUS LLAMA BURGER!
YOU SICKO!
I LIKE THAT.

WHAT ELSE?
YOU MEAN ME?
OKAY, UM . . . NO PETS. NO HOBBIES, UNLESS YOU COUNT KNITTING, WHICH I PRETTY MUCH SUCK AT.
ME TOO.
YOU KNIT?
BADLY.
AND JUST WITH REGULAR YARN, NOT LLAMAS OR ANYTHING.
THAT'S GOOD.
UM . . .

I LIKE MUSIC AND . . .
SUNSETS?
OH YES, SUNSETS AND LONG WALKS ON THE BEACH . . .
HOW'S YOUR PERSONAL RELATIONSHIP WITH THE LORD?
I'D HAVE TO SAY IT'S PRETTY MUCH IMPERSONAL.
DON'T TELL MAGGIE KWAN.
HEY, WHAT HAPPENED TO FREEDOM OF SPEECH?
NOTHING. MAGGIE'S JUST A BIT FUZZY ON FREEDOM OF RELIGION.
CHECK OUT PEANUT BUTTER CUP.
GETTING MIGHTY COZY WITH OL' DOOKIE SUZUKI.
OOH, MAYBE HE'LL WRITE HER A LETTER ON HIS EXTRA-SPECIAL HELLO KITTY STATIONERY!

A FEW NIGHTS LATER
PING!
MOM
SO . . .
GIVE AWAY

YOU'RE KEEPING YOUR CARDS PRETTY CLOSE TO YOUR CHEST CONCERNING YOUR NEW SCHOOL.
I LIKE IT.
YOU DO?
YEAH.
MY HOMEROOM TEACHER'S A TRIP. HIS SUBJECT IS ALGEBRA, BUT HE TALKS LIKE AN ENGLISH TEACHER.
I WAS AN UTTER DISASTER WHEN IT CAME TO ALGEBRA.
THERE'S THIS GIRL NAMED LOUANN, AND A GUY NAMED DAVID . . .
SEE?
I KNEW YOU'D FIND YOUR GANG!
AND THIS OTHER GUY, ZOO.
ZOO?
IT'S REALLY CHRISTOPHER, BUT HE LIKES ZOO BETTER.

HMM. ZOO. I ONCE HAD QUITE A THING FOR A BOY NAMED BIRD.
FASCINATING.
IS HE CUTE, THIS ZOO?
GOD, MOM! I HAVEN'T NOTICED, OKAY?
HEE HEE. METHINKS THE LADY DOTH PROTEST TOO MUCH.
WHAT'S THIS WE'RE EATING, ANYWAY?
MMFF?
GADO-GADO.
EXCUSE ME?
IT'S FROM THAT COOKBOOK THE MILLERS BROUGHT US FROM BALI. REMEMBER WHEN WE WATCHED THEIR CAT?

AW, I MISS MY LITTLE SNOWBALL.
UGH! THAT WHITE FUR GETTING ALL OVER EVERYTHING.
GIVE
C'MON, SNOWBALL ROCKED.
THAT ANIMAL'S BRAIN WAS THE SIZE OF A WALNUT.
YEAH, BUT SO'S A DINOSAUR'S AND THEY'RE LIKE 400 TIMES SNOWBALL'S SIZE.
YOU HAVE A POINT.
YES!
YOU LIKE?
YEAH. ESPECIALLY THIS SAUCE STUFF.

YOU WON'T BELIEVE ME WHEN I TELL YOU HOW EASY IT WAS.
YOU TAKE A LITTLE BIT OF GINGER . . .
mom TV
A LITTLE BIT OF GARLIC . . .
mom TV
A COUPLE TEASPOONS OF SOY SAUCE . . .
A HALF CUP OF PEANUT BUTTER . . .
DUMP EVERYTHING IN THE BLENDER AND . . .
mom TV
. . . VOILÀ!
WWWWRRRRR!

TAKE THE LEFTOVERS WITH YOU FOR LUNCH TOMORROW IF YOU WANT.
THAT'S OKAY.
I BET IT'D MAKE A GOOD DIP FOR RAW VEGGIES.
YEAH, BUT . . .
I THINK ZOO'S BRINGING A QUICHE FOR EVERYBODY TO SHARE.
HE LIKES TO BAKE.
OOOOH, ZOO!
MO-O-OM!
OKAY, OKAY!
SO, WHAT DO YOU HEAR FROM THE OLD CEDARWOOD CROWD?
NOTHING.

REALLY?
WELL, YOU'VE PROBABLY ALL GOT YOUR HANDS FULL WITH THE START OF THE SCHOOL YEAR . . .
I JUST THOUGHT MAYBE YOU WOULD HAVE SPOKEN TO CHERYL OR DEANNA OR ONE OF THAT BUNCH.
NOPE.
I LEFT A COUPLE OF MESSAGES FOR CHERYL BUT SHE HASN'T CALLED BACK.
WELL . . .
I'LL BET SHE'S JUST WAITING FOR THE DUST TO SETTLE.
IT'S A BUSY TIME FOR EVERYONE.
YES. YOU SAID THAT ALREADY.

NOT THIS WEEKEND, BUT MAYBE THE ONE AFTER, WE COULD ARRANGE A TRIP TO THE OLD STOMPING GROUNDS.
MAYBE WORK IT SO I'D DROP YOU AT CHERYL'S ON SATURDAY, AND HER DAD COULD DRIVE YOU BACK SUNDAY.
I'M NOT GOING TO INVITE MYSELF OVER!
I DIDN'T MEAN THAT—
IT'S NO BIG DEAL, OKAY? I'M HAPPY HANGING WITH MY NEW FRIENDS.
MY LIFE IS HERE NOW, RIGHT?
RIGHT!
I THINK IT'S GREAT THE WAY YOU'RE JUMPING IN WITH BOTH FEET.
MEANING?
OH, YOU KNOW, JUST THAT YOU'RE GETTING OUT THERE, AND MAKING NEW FRIENDS,
AND NOT MOONING AROUND BECAUSE YOU'RE NOT BACK IN CEDARWOOD.
GGGGG
WELL, YEAH. DUH.

DUH!
DOY!
DUH!
DUR!
DUHHH!
OKAY, I'M GOING TO GET A MIRROR SO YOU CAN SEE YOURSELF.
PLEASE DON'T.
YOU LOOK LIKE—
A SUPERMODEL!
THAT'S NOT WHAT I WAS GOING TO SAY.

OCTOBER

I GUESS IT WAS PRETTY OBVIOUS THAT ZOO AND I WERE DESTINED TO BE MORE THAN FRIENDS.

PCHS

Hey Peanut,
Only 5 minutes till final bell.
Good thing cuz I'm about to
croak from missing you
Zoo

AH, MS. WILDHACK, THE VERY PERSON I WAS LOOKING FOR!
WE HAVE SERIOUS BUSINESS TO ATTEND TO.
MISS ANDERSON'S IN A BIT OF A KERFUFFLE THAT SHE WASN'T ALERTED TO YOUR CONDITION.
MISS ANDERSON?
SCHOOL NURSE. APPARENTLY THE GRAPEVINE'S NOT HER PREFERRED ORGAN FOR LEARNING THAT A STUDENT HAS A SERIOUS ALLERGY.
THERE WAS ALSO SOMETHING ABOUT SOME SPECIALIZED PIECE OF EQUIPMENT SHOULD YOU SUFFER AN ATTACK DURING SCHOOL HOURS—
SOME SORT OF PEN-SHAPED DEVICE?
OHHH, RIGHT, MY EPIPEN!
MOST LIKELY. I CAN'T KEEP THESE THINGS STRAIGHT.
MISS ANDERSON HAS QUITE THE COLLECTION OF STUDENT MEDICATIONS THERE IN HER OFFICE.

WAIT, SHE WANTS ME TO GIVE IT TO HER?
I ASSUME THAT'S WHY SHE BROUGHT IT UP.
BUT THE NURSE AT MY OLD SCHOOL SAID IT WAS OKAY IF I . . .
I MEAN, I'VE ONLY GOT ONE PEN . . . AND THEY'RE KIND OF EXPENSIVE.
IF THEFT IS A CONCERN, I CAN ASSURE YOU THAT SUCH A DEVICE IS MUCH SAFER IN MISS ANDERSON'S LOCKED CABINET THAN IN SOME UNTENDED BACKPACK.
YEAH, BUT I'M PRETTY CAREFUL . . .
OH YES, WE'RE ALL PRETTY CAREFUL . . .

TRUE STORY, BY THE WAY.
THE THING IS, I'M REALLY, REALLY CAREFUL.
I SHOULD HOPE SO, GIVEN THE SEVERITY OF YOUR CONDITION.
BUT REALLY, MS. WILDHACK, THIS IS A CONVERSATION FOR YOU TO BE HAVING WITH THE NURSE.
SHE WON'T BE THERE NOW, BUT SHE REQUESTS THAT YOU COME SEE HER IN HER OFFICE AT YOUR EARLIEST CONVENIENCE.
APPARENTLY YOU'RE ALSO MISSING SOME CRUCIAL HEALTH FORM, THE ONE YOU WERE TO HAVE RETURNED ON THE SECOND DAY OF SCHOOL.
BUT I TURNED THAT IN ALREADY. AT LEAST, I THINK I DID.
MISS ANDERSON LOOKED IN THE FILES, AND IT'S NOT THERE.
OH WAIT, WAS MY MOM SUPPOSED TO SIGN IT OR SOMETHING?

YES, CHECK WITH YOUR MOTHER. DESPITE OUR BEST INTENTIONS, THESE THINGS OFTEN WIND UP BURIED BENEATH A MOUNTAIN OF PAPERWORK.
YEAH, MY MOM'S DESK IS REALLY MESSY.
ALTERNATIVELY, YOU COULD ASK THAT MISS ANDERSON GIVE YOU A REPLACEMENT FORM WHEN YOU SEE HER TOMORROW.
OKAY.
GOOD. YOU HAVE MY PERMISSION TO TEND TO THIS MATTER FIRST THING, AFTER WHICH I'LL EXPECT YOU TO JOIN US IN HOMEROOM.
S'ALRIGHT?
S'ALRIGHT.
AND SPEND SOME TIME GOING OVER TODAY'S EQUATIONS. WE'LL BE HAVING A LITTLE QUIZ ON FRIDAY!

LATER THAT DAY . . .
SLAM!
CAN I HAVE DINNER ON A TRAY TONIGHT? MR. LARCH JUST LOADED A TON OF HOMEWORK ON TOP OF TWO HUMONGOUS TESTS I'VE GOT TOMORROW.
JEEZ, THEY REALLY PILE IT ON. IT CAN'T BE HEALTHY.
Eppy Pen
Eppy Pen
Did you mean: EpiPen
Home Page - EpiPen
skip to primary nav
How to use EpiPen
EPIPEN
ABOUT EPIPEN
Auto-Injector
EpiPen
EPIPEN 2-Pak

POP
POP
POP
TAP TAP
BLEEBLEEP!
H'LO?

HEY!
. . .
UM, IT'S ME.
OH SORRY, I DIDN'T RECOGNIZE YOUR VOICE.
THAT'S OKAY . . . SO . . . WHAT'S GOING ON?
UM . . . NOTHING MUCH. WHEN WAS THE LAST TIME WE TALKED?
YOU WERE DOING THAT AIDS WALK THING—
OH YEAH. THAT WAS LIKE A MILLION YEARS AGO!
I KNOW.
YOU SHOULD'VE SEEN!

DANIEL MARCH AND FREDDY LANGDON AND, LIKE, SIX OTHER GUYS WENT IN HULA OUTFITS!
WE TRIED TO MAKE THEM GO IN REGULAR DRAG, LIKE OUR DRESSES OR WHATEVER—
WALK FOR CURE
CURE HIV
CURE HIV
WHY?
JUST TO BE FUNNY. I'M LIKE, "FREDDY, NO ONE'S GOING TO THINK YOU'RE GAY!"
I PRACTICALLY HAD TO SIT ON HIM!
HA . . . WHEN DID YOU START HANGING OUT WITH FREDDY LANGDON?
UM, I GUESS . . . HEATHER PAIGE HAD THIS PARTY AND FREDDY AND I STARTED MAKING FUN OF THIS RIDICULOUS CHAIR IN THE REC ROOM. IT WAS LIKE A THRONE OR SOMETHING.
HEATHER *PAIGE*?

I KNOW YOU THINK SHE'S A B, BUT SHE'S ACTUALLY REALLY COOL.
UM . . . OKAY.
SOOOO . . .
OH YEAH. I ALMOST FORGOT. I HAVE SOMETHING KIND OF . . . DORKY TO TELL YOU.
YOU'RE GONNA THINK I'VE GONE INSANE OR SOMETHING—
HOLD ON A SEC.
WHAT?!?
I'M ON THE PHONE!!!

I'VE GOT TO GO. MY MOM'S HAVING A CONNIPTION BECAUSE I'VE GOT A BUTTLOAD OF HOMEWORK.
OH . . . YEAH, I SHOULD GET STARTED ON MINE, TOO.
SO, I GUESS, THANKS FOR CALLING AND ALL.
SURE, NO PROBLEMA.
HAVE FUN WITH ALL YOUR SHALLOW, HOMOPHOBIC FRIENDS!

POP
UM, SO, THERE'S SOMETHING I NEED TO GET OFF MY CHEST.
THIS IS GOING TO SOUND WEIRD, BUT THE THING IS . . .

I DON'T REALLY HAVE A—
I'M NOT SURE I WANT TO HEAR THIS.
I KNOW, ME EITHER.
IT'S JUST THAT YOU REPRESENTED YOURSELF TO US IN A CERTAIN WAY . . .
AND IF IT TURNS OUT YOU'RE SOMETHING DIFFERENT . . .
IT'S OKAY. I FORGET WHAT I WAS GOING TO SAY.
POP
POP

SO? DID YOU REMEMBER?
REMEMBER WHAT?
WHATEVER IT WAS YOU WERE ABOUT TO SAY?
ANGELA, DON'T TAKE THIS THE WRONG WAY, BUT I'M NOT REALLY THAT GOOD FRIENDS WITH YOU.
POP
YOUR HOMEROOM TEACHER IS THE ONE TO WHOM YOU'LL COME WHEN—
HELL FREEZES OVER.
IS THAT HOW WE MEET OFFERS OF EMOTIONAL SUPPORT? WITH MOCKERY AND INGRATITUDE?
NO, WAIT, MR. LARCH—
HRRUMPH!
POP

I'M SORRY. I CAN'T SPILL THE BEANS. AT LEAST NOT YET.
SURE YOU CAN, PEANUT.
I HAVE NO IDEA WHAT I'M DOING . . .
GOOD LUCK!
BEEB BEEB
POP

DIRECTORY ASSISTANCE. WHAT LISTING, PLEASE?
PLAINFIELD RESIDENTIAL. SUZUKI.
HI, YOU'VE REACHED THE SUZUKIS! WE'RE NOT HOME, SO LEAVE A MESSAGE AND KAZUO, MARGE, OR CHRIS WILL CALL YOU RIGHT BACK!
MOAN . . . !
CLICK
KNOCK
KNOCK
DO YOU WANT ME TO CALL THE PRINCIPAL? BECAUSE I REALLY FEEL THIS WORKLOAD IS EXCESSIVE.

IT'S NOT KINDERGARTEN!
I DON'T NEED MY MOMMY CHARGING IN TO—
ALL RIGHT. BUT IF IT KEEPS ON THIS WAY—
IT WON'T. IT'S JUST THAT I HAVE TWO TESTS TO STUDY FOR.
WHAT'S THIS?
I THOUGHT WE'D SWORN OFF THE INTERNET!
DON'T TELL ME ZOO'S FALLEN OFF THE WAGON, TOO!
IT'S RESEARCH.
AND HE HASN'T "FALLEN OFF THE WAGON." HE DOES HIS RESEARCH AT THE LIBRARY.
UH-HUH.
YOU'RE SURE THERE'S NOT SOME TOP-SECRET HOTMAIL ACCOUNT THAT ONLY THE TWO OF YOU KNOW ABOUT?
RRRNH!!!

ALL RIGHT! DON'T HAVE A COW! I'M GETTING OUT OF YOUR HAIR RIGHT NOW!
WAIT, MOM, DO YOU KNOW ANYTHING ABOUT EE-PINE-FRINE?
EE-PINE-FRINE?
I'M DOING A PROJECT FOR MR. LARCH. WE'RE DIVIDED INTO TEAMS. EACH TEAM'S RESEARCHING A DIFFERENT MEDICAL CONDITION.
I THOUGHT MR. LARCH WAS ALGEBRA.
HE IS, BUT BECAUSE HE'S HOMEROOM, HE HAS TO DO HEALTH, TOO.
IN MY DAY, HEALTH WAS A EUPHEMISM FOR SEX ED.
IT'S STILL THAT, BUT ALSO REGULAR-TYPE STUFF ABOUT BODIES AND, UM, HEALTH.
YOU'D THINK THEY'D LEAVE THAT FOR BIOLOGY.
OHHHH. EPINEPHRINE. NO WONDER I DIDN'T KNOW WHAT YOU WERE TALKING ABOUT.

IT'S EPPY-NEFF-RIN, NOT EE-PINE-FRINE.
WELL, HOW WAS I SUPPOSED TO KNOW?
DID YOUR TEAM GET ASTHMA?
NO, ALLERGIES.
REALLY? I THOUGHT EPINEPHRINE HAD TO DO WITH THOSE INHALER THINGAMAJIGS FOR PEOPLE WITH ASTHMA.
I'M PRETTY SURE THAT'S SOMETHING ELSE.
LET'S SEE.
"NUMBER ONE DOCTOR-PRESCRIBED TREATMENT FOR THOSE WITH A HISTORY OF ANAPHYLAXIS"— WHATEVER THAT MEANS.
IT'S WHEN YOUR THROAT SWELLS SHUT.
OOF, JIMMY STACKHOUSE HAD THAT. REMEMBER JIMMY FROM NURSERY SCHOOL?
NO.
WELL, IN THAT CASE, YOU'RE PROBABLY NOT GOING TO REMEMBER THE PICNIC THE SCHOOL HAD FOR ALL THE FAMILIES. . . .
I WAS THREE!

IT WAS TO CELEBRATE THE END OF THE YEAR, AND THIS LITTLE JIMMY STACKHOUSE—HE WAS SO CUTE, ARE YOU SURE YOU DON'T REMEMBER HIM?
MOM!
ALL RIGHT! SO, MIDWAY THROUGH THIS PICNIC, JIMMY GOT STUNG BY SOME SORT OF BEE. NOBODY SAW IT HAPPEN, BUT ALL OF A SUDDEN HIS EYES SWELLED SHUT. . . .
HIS FACE PUFFED UP LIKE THIS.
IT WAS LIKE HE WAS BEING STRANGLED.
GOD, THAT'S SCARY.
YES, IT WAS.
WHAT HAPPENED?
OH, IT WAS PANDEMONIUM, EVERYONE RUNNING AROUND TRYING TO FIGURE OUT WHAT TO DO, TRYING TO KEEP THE REST OF YOU KIDS CALM.
ONE MOTHER HAD THE GOOD SENSE TO RUN TO THE NEAREST HOUSE AND ASK THEM TO CALL 911.
THIS WAS BEFORE CELL PHONES?

THEY MAY HAVE JUST COME OUT. YOUR FATHER HAD THIS BIG CLUNKY PHONE IN HIS CAR, BUT BACK THEN BEEPERS WERE THE THING THAT EVERYBODY HAD.
MM. I CAN STILL SEE SHEILA DORSEY TEARING TOWARD THIS LITTLE RED HOUSE ACROSS THE PARK.
AFTER A WHILE THE AMBULANCE CAME AND TOOK JIMMY AWAY. LATER WE FOUND OUT HE WAS ALLERGIC TO BEE STINGS. NOBODY KNEW, BECAUSE HE'D NEVER BEEN STUNG BEFORE.
AMBUL
911
DID HE DIE?
GOODNESS NO! THEY WERE ABLE TO GIVE HIM SOMETHING THAT STOPPED THE REACTION RIGHT AWAY.
EPINEPHRINE?
I THINK IT MUST'VE BEEN. THAT'S WHAT MADE ME THINK OF HIM, AT ANY RATE.
I THINK THAT'S WHAT IT DOES, STOPS STUFF LIKE THAT.
WE'RE BLESSED TO BE LIVING IN AN AGE OF MODERN MEDICINE.

SO, WAIT, DO YOU KNOW, IS IT THE KIND OF THING YOU CAN JUST WALK INTO A STORE AND BUY?
EPINEPHRINE? I WOULDN'T THINK SO.
I CAN'T IMAGINE WHAT ANYONE WITHOUT A LEGITIMATE NEED WOULD WANT WITH IT, BUT THERE ARE SO MANY LAWSUITS THESE DAYS. ALL IT TAKES IS ONE DOPEY KID LOOKING FOR A NOVEL WAY TO GET HIGH. . . .
OH SURE, YOU KNOW US KIDS. ALWAYS LOOKING FOR NEW WAYS TO GET HIGH. . . .
DIG AROUND ONLINE. I'LL BET THERE'S A MILLION THINGS ABOUT IT THERE. . . .
GOOD LUCK!
THANKS.
GRRR!
STUPID, STUPID, STUPID!
SQUEEK!
FLOP!

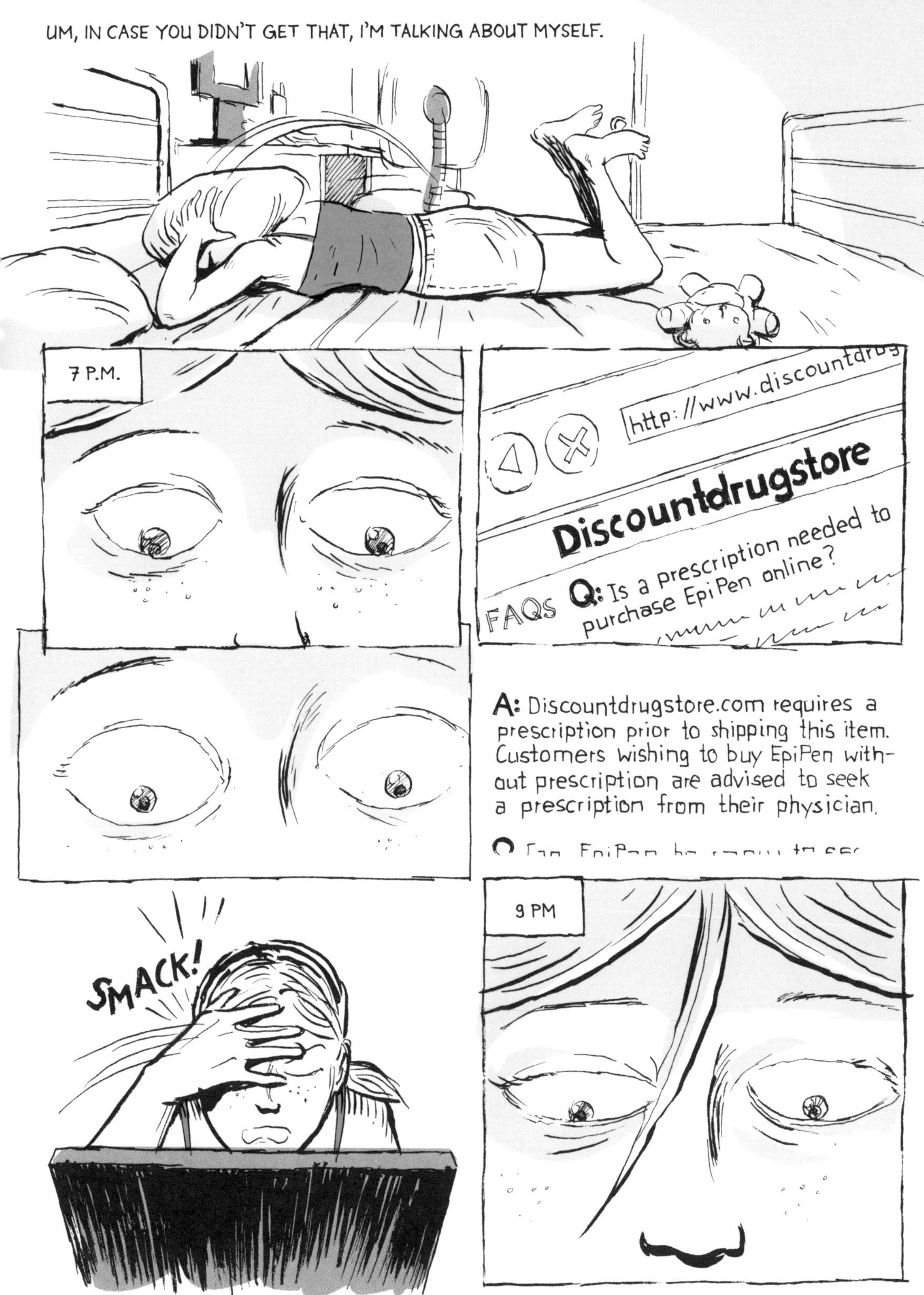
UM, IN CASE YOU DIDN'T GET THAT, I'M TALKING ABOUT MYSELF.
7 P.M.
http://www.discountdrug
Discountdrugstore
FAQS Q: Is a prescription needed to purchase EpiPen online?
A: Discountdrugstore.com requires a prescription prior to shipping this item. Customers wishing to buy EpiPen without prescription are advised to seek a prescription from their physician.
SMACK!
9 PM

Article IVc: Pediatric Review Committee's Findings in Eastern District Survey
A total of 79 respondents require an Epinephrine Administration Form to be completed by school nurse following any situation requiring the use of epinephrine during the school day.
NEXT
72% of students with known allergies supplied a backup EpiPen to the health office. In all but one reported incident, the school nurse administered the epinephrine. In the other incident, the student self-administered. Parents were notified in 100% of the incidents.
KFFT!
11 P.M.
West Jolene Bugle
sunny 63 F
West Jolene County's most trusted News Source
Hero Crossing Guard Rescues Kindergartner from Deadly Snack Mishap
West Jolene Schools employee Myra Yaeger has no formal medical training, but that didn't stop the grandmother of three from saving the day when she noticed young Tiffany Martinez, age 5, with a peanut the child discovered on the sidewalk. "I didn't know about the allergy thing," Mrs. Yaeger recalled modestly, in the hours after the near tragedy. "But I always tell kids not to eat things they find on the ground."

1 A.M.
HEE...
YOUTUBE
HI, I'M CASSIE CLAYBORNE, HERE WITH ANOTHER CHANNEL 6 HEALTH BREAK!
TODAY WE'LL LEARN HOW TO USE AN EPIPEN TO STOP AN ALLERGIC REACTION. . . .
FOR A REAL ALLERGIC REACTION, I'D INJECT THIS DIRECTLY INTO MY THIGH, BUT SINCE I'M NOT ALLERGIC—
AND THIS NEEDLE LOOKS REALLY BIG—
I'M GOING TO DEMONSTRATE ON THIS TOMATO.
SPLOSH!
OH MY GOD! HA HA HA! I'M SORRY! CAN WE DO A RESHOOT?

5:59 A.M.
6 A.M.
BBRRRRRAAAAAAAAAAAAANNGG...
6:00
WHUH?!!! . . . OH NO.
MOMMY? I DON'T FEEL SO WELL.
DID YOU TAKE YOUR TEMPERATURE?
NO, BUT . . .
I'LL GET THE THERMOMETER. YOU KNOW THE RULES.

I USED TO FAKE SICK A LOT SO I COULD STAY HOME AND WATCH CARTOONS.

AFTER A WHILE MOM GOT WISE AND DECLARED I COULD ONLY MISS SCHOOL IF I WAS RUNNING A FEVER.
OPEN.

I'D RUN THE THERMOMETER UNDER HOT WATER, HOLD IT UP TO A LIGHTBULB. SHE ALWAYS FIGURED IT OUT.
KEEP IT UNDER YOUR TONGUE UNTIL IT BEEPS.

BEEBEEBEEBEE

98.3°.

LOOKS LIKE AN ACUTE CASE OF TWO-TEST-ITIS TO ME.

HAVE A NICE DAY!
PCHS
SADIE!
HEY, PEANUT!
UH-OH. WHAT'S WRONG?
TELL HIM! TELL HIM!
NOTHING. JUST PISSY, THAT'S ALL.

AW, POOR PEANUT.
HEY! I KNOW SOMETHING THAT'LL MAKE YOU FEEL BETTER!
SMECK!
I'VE GOT TO SEE THE NURSE.
OH NO, YOU'RE SICK?
NOT REALLY.
FEMALE TROUBLES.
WANT ME TO TELL LARCH, SO HE WON'T MARK YOU LATE?
IT'S OKAY. HE ALREADY KNOWS.
I CAN GET YOUR HOMEWORK ASSIGNMENTS IF YOU NEED ME TO!
PCHS

NURSE
KNOCK KNOCK
COME ON IN!
MISS ANDERSON?
PLEASE! CALL ME NURSE ANDY. EVERYONE ELSE DOES. RIGHT, KEVIN?
WAH-WUNH.
AH-AH-AH! UNDER THE TONGUE FOR THE FULL TWENTY SECONDS.

NOW, WHAT CAN I DO FOR YOU, HON?
I'M SADIE WILDHACK. MR. LARCH SAID—
MY AWOL PEANUT ALLERGY! GOOD TO FINALLY MEET YOU!
MR. LARCH SAID I'M SUPPOSED TO GIVE YOU AN EPIPEN, BUT—
BEEBEEBEEBE
WHOOPSADAISY, YOUR FRIES ARE UP!
OH, HONEY, YOU ARE ONE SICK PUP. IS MOM OR DAD AROUND TO COME PICK YOU UP?
MY MOM.
OKEYDOKE, WRITE HER NUMBER ON THIS PAD. YOU CAN HANG OUT ON THE COUCH TILL SHE GETS HERE.
ONE SEC.

HELLO, MRS. JANOWSKI? THIS IS NURSE ANDERSON OVER AT PCHS.
I'M AFRAID KEVIN'S STILL A BIT URPY. . . .
VITAMINS
OKAY, KID, SHE'S ON HER WAY.
NOW THEN, WHERE WERE WE?
WELL, MR. LARCH SAID YOU'RE MISSING MY HEALTH FORM . . .
. . . AND ALSO, YOU WERE UPSET ABOUT THE EPIPEN?
OH, THAT HOWARD!

I LOVE HIM TO DEATH, BUT HE DRIVES ME ABSOLUTELY CUCKOO-BANANAS!
I'VE NEVER MET A BIGGER DRAMA QUEEN!
FOR THE RECORD, I WASN'T UPSET, I WAS . . . CONCERNED.
I LIKE ALL MY DUCKS IN A ROW. THAT WAY, WHEN THE OFFICE CALLS TO SAY, "SO-AND-SO JUST COLLAPSED IN THE LUNCHROOM," I HAVE SOME IDEA OF WHAT WE'RE DEALING WITH.
(MOAN . . .)
UH-OH, KEVIN, YOU NEED THE BARF BUCKET?
UH-UH.
ALL RIGHT, JUST TRY TO GIVE ME A WARNING IF YOU DO. JOSÉ JUST MOPPED THESE FLOORS.
SO, BACK TO YOU, I SEE YOU'RE WEARING A MED-ALERT. THAT'S GOOD.
OH . . . YEAH.

DO YOU CARRY YOUR EPIPEN WITH YOU AT ALL TIMES?
UH-HUH.
AND YOU KNOW HOW TO USE IT?
UH-HUH.
YOU SEE? THAT'S ALL I NEEDED TO KNOW!
YOU DON'T WANT ME TO BRING ONE IN?
I'VE GOT MY STASH.
IT'S NOT LIKE YOU'RE SOME HELPLESS KINDERGARTNER. LET ME TELL YOU, I WORKED IN AN ELEMENTARY SCHOOL.
THOSE LITTLE KIDS ARE SWEET, BUT THEY CAN BARELY MANAGE TO WIPE THEIR OWN NOSES.
I HAD TO DO EVERYTHING FOR THEM, AND I MEAN EV-ER-Y-THING!

I MEAN, OBVIOUSLY, YOU CAN'T LET A 7-YEAR-OLD RUN AROUND WITH AN EPIPEN. FIRST CHANCE HE GETS, HE'S GONNA STICK IT IN HIS BEST FRIEND'S EYE—
UNH!
SEE? NOW YOU KNOW WHY I PREFER TEENAGERS! YOU GUYS CAN ACTUALLY TAKE CARE OF YOURSELVES.
I'M HERE IF YOU NEED ME, BUT AS FAR AS YOUR PEANUT THING GOES, I'M ASSUMING YOU KNOW THE DRILL BY NOW.
DEFINITELY.
LEAVE IT TO HOWARD TO MAKE A MOUNTAIN OUT OF A, I DON'T KNOW WHAT, A MOSQUITO BITE.
HE PROBABLY HAD YOU THINKING I WAS SOME SORT OF A CRAZED LUNATIC WOMAN.
KIND OF.
LISTEN, YOU GO BACK TO THAT HOMEROOM OF YOURS AND TELL MR. LARCH THAT NURSE ANDY'S FIXING TO BOX HIS EARS.
HA HA. OKAY.
HOLD ON A SEC, I'LL WRITE YOU A PASS.
AND LET ME RUSTLE UP ONE OF THOSE DUMB HEALTH FORMS, TOO. FILL IT OUT, GET MOM TO GIVE IT HER JOHN HANCOCK, AND WE'RE DONE.
I'LL ASK HER TONIGHT.

DANG, MAN, MR. MCCLOSKEY TOLD YOU TO WEAR PROTECTIVE GOGGLES!
ARRGGGHNNG . . .
WAY TO BE AN ANUS, DARRIN. CAN'T YOU SEE HE'S REALLY HURT?
Yay! Peanut's back! What kind of drugs did that nurse give you? You're like an entirely different person!
xxoo Zoo
HIP HIP HOORAY!!! SADIE'S OK!

LUNCH . . .
PENNY FOR YOUR THOUGHTS.
TELL HIM, TELL HIM, TELL HIM.
NOTHING.
C'MON.
IT'S STUPID.
I SERIOUSLY DOUBT THAT.

OKAY, UM, I WAS THINKING ABOUT . . .
"THIS TOTALLY UNFUNNY COMEDIAN GUY . . ."
"IF GETTING A TATTOO REMOVED HURTS WORSE THAN GETTING A TATTOO . . ."
"HOW MAGICIANS DO THAT TRICK WHERE THEY SAW THE LADY IN HALF . . ."
"GLOBAL WARMING . . ."
"HOW NOBODY ELSE'S BOYFRIEND THINKS CELL PHONES ARE EVIL . . ."
POP
BINGO!
"HOW NOBODY ELSE'S BOYFRIEND THINKS CELL PHONES ARE EVIL . . ."
POP
POP
WHAT IF I NEEDED TO GET HOLD OF YOU IN AN EMERGENCY?

YOU MEAN LIKE THE TWIN TOWERS OR SOMETHING?
NO, NOT THAT. . . .
BECAUSE I JUST WANT TO BE STRAIGHT WITH YOU, WHEN PLAINFIELD COMES UNDER TERRORIST SIEGE, I'M GOING TO COLLAPSE IN A TERRIFIED, SNIVELING HEAP.
OH NO, YOU'RE NOT COUNTING ON *ME* TO RESCUE *YOU*?
GOOD POINT. ON SECOND THOUGHT, WHEN THE TERRORISTS ATTACK, I'M MORPHING INTO A TOTAL HE-MAN!
"SIT TIGHT, LITTLE LADY! I'M COMING TO RESCUE YOU!"
HOW?
ON HORSEBACK!
HA HA, VERY FUNNY. FOR REAL, THOUGH, WHAT IF YOU DIDN'T KNOW WHERE I WAS?
WOULD YOU BORROW SOMEBODY'S PHONE? OR AT LEAST SEND AN EMAIL ASKING IF ANYONE'S SEEN ME?

WHAT? YOU DON'T THINK WE'RE CAPABLE OF TELEPATHY?
WHEN THE BOMBS START FALLING . . .
. . . YOU JUST CLOSE YOUR EYES TIGHT AND THINK, "ZOO!"
I'M SERIOUS.
SO AM I.
NO YOU'RE NOT, YOU'RE CLOWNING AROUND.
I TRIED TO CALL YOU LAST NIGHT, BY THE WAY.
YOU DID?
NUTRI BAR
THE MESSAGE ANSWERED, SO I HUNG UP.
WHY DID YOU CALL ME?
BECAUSE I WANTED TO TALK TO YOU?
OH.

I WANT TO TALK TO YOU, TOO, PEANUT, JUST . . . NOT ON THE PHONE.
I LIKE BEING ABLE TO SEE YOUR FACE WHEN WE TALK.
IN THAT CASE, MAYBE YOU SHOULD GET A LAPTOP WITH A BUILT-IN CAMERA.
IT'S POSSIBLE TO CALL PEOPLE FROM YOUR COMPUTER THESE DAYS.
AND IT'S FREE.
UM, YEAH. THAT'S PROBABLY NOT GOING TO HAPPEN.
RIGHT. WHAT IF WE REALLY NEED TO GET IN TOUCH WITH EACH OTHER, THOUGH?
CANDY
YOU DON'T LIKE MY NOTES?
ARE YOU KIDDING? I'VE KEPT EVERY SINGLE ONE!
BUT WHAT ARE YOU GOING TO DO IF . . . IF SOMEONE OPENS FIRE IN THE LIBRARY OR SOMETHING?
DON'T SAY THAT.

HOP ON YOUR BIKE?
WRITE A LITTLE NOTE THAT SAYS "HIDE UNDER THE TABLE"?
I'M SORRY.
I DIDN'T MEAN THAT AS SNOTTY AS IT CAME OUT.
I'M JUST . . . STRESSED. I DON'T KNOW WHY.
WHY DIDN'T YOU LEAVE A MESSAGE?
WHY WOULD I, WHEN YOUR MORAL CODE OR WHATEVER PROHIBITS YOU FROM CALLING ME BACK?

MY "MORAL CODE OR WHATEVER"?
ALL I'M SAYING IS, IT'S NOT ABNORMAL TO USE THE PHONE NOW AND THEN.
OH GREAT, NOW YOU'RE MAD.
FORGIVE ME IF I'M WRONG, BUT I'M PRETTY SURE, IN YOUR HEART, YOU KNOW MY FEELINGS ABOUT "MODERN COMMUNICATIONS" AREN'T JUST ME BEING WEIRD FOR WEIRDNESS' SAKE.
I DO. I DO, BUT—
I'D ALSO LIKE TO THINK YOU KNOW HOW I FEEL ABOUT YOU.
I DO.
SO WHY ARE YOU MAKING A MOUNTAIN OUT OF A—

BUT ZOO, WHAT IF IT'S AN EMERGENCY?
WAS IT?
IS THAT WHY YOU HAD TO SEE THE NURSE TODAY? YOU WERE HAVING AN EMERGENCY THAT ONLY ME PICKING UP THE PHONE COULD HAVE PREVENTED?
I RESPECT YOUR BELIEFS. WHY CAN'T YOU RESPECT MINE?
I DO!
OKAY, THEN WHAT ARE WE FIGHTING ABOUT?
PLEASE TELL ME YOU'RE NOT GIVING ME THE SILENT TREATMENT.

ARRRGH! THAT CELIA WILSON IS SUCH A HEIFER!
DID YOU HEAR WHAT SHE SAID ABOUT DAVID?
UM . . . UH-UH, NO.
SWEAR TO GOD, IF THAT WENCH COMES WITHIN TEN FEET OF ME, I'LL RIP HER EARRINGS OUT!
NICE LUNCH, LOU.
SO? I CRAVE JUNK FOOD WHEN I'M PISSED OFF! I CAN'T HELP IT! IT CALMS ME DOWN.
WHAT DID CELIA SAY ABOUT DAVID?
SHE SAID HE WAS DOING THAT THING . . .

THAT THING WHERE A GUY TIES A ROPE AROUND HIS NECK TO HEIGHTEN THE SENSATION WHEN HE'S . . .
YOU KNOW . . .
CHOKING HIS CHICKEN?
YOU MEAN LIKE THAT KID FROM WESTBROOK?
THE ONE WHO *DIED.*
THAT'S TERRIBLE!
SO, WAS HE?
WAS HE WHAT?
THAT IS SO NOT FUNNY, ZOO! HOW'D YOU LIKE IT IF CELIA WENT AROUND TALKING CRAP LIKE THAT ABOUT YOU?
WELL, NUMBER ONE, I'M SURE SHE DOES. . . .

AND NUMBER TWO, WHO'S GOING TO BELIEVE HER? UNLESS OF COURSE, SHE'S CLAIMING TO BE AN EYEWITNESS.
THAT WOULD BE SO AWESOME. LET'S START A RUMOR SAYING SHE WAS THERE, TOO!
SADIE, THINK! THAT'S THE SAME AS SAYING HER STUPID STORY IS TRUE!
YECHH, WHAT'S IN THESE THINGS? TASTES LIKE SQUID ON A STICK!
HEE HEE, SQUID ON A STICK.
YOU JEST, BUT IF WE WERE IN JAPAN, YOU'D—
OH SHIT!!!

DON'T EAT THAT!!!
WHAT? OH MY GOD, WHAT???
THAT CHIP HAD PEANUT OIL IN IT!
OH GOD, WHAT DO WE DO?
IT'S OKAY, I SPIT IT OUT! I SPIT IT OUT!
ARE YOU SURE YOU GOT IT ALL?
I'LL GET THE NURSE!
DON'T!
SADIE!

YOU SHOULD GET HER PEN.
OKAY!
I DON'T NEED IT!
IS SHE ALL RIGHT?
SHE'S ALLERGIC TO PEANUTS AND SHE ATE SOMETHING WITH PEANUT OIL!
WHOA! YOU WANT ME TO FIND A TEACHER?
PLEASE DON'T! IT'S ONLY BAD IF I SWALLOW SOME, AND I DIDN'T SWALLOW ANY!
YOU CAN'T KNOW THAT, THOUGH.
JUST ONE LITTLE CRUMB—
I PROMISE YOU, IF I WAS HAVING A REACTION, YOU'D KNOW.
WHAT ABOUT YOUR EPIPEN?
WHAT ABOUT IT?
I FEEL SO GUILTY.
IT'S NOT YOUR FAULT. IT'S MINE FOR NOT CHECKING THE LABEL.

I'D FEEL MORE COMFORTABLE IF YOU'D LET US CALL THE NURSE.
CAN WE PLEASE FORGET IT? C'MON. EVERYBODY'S LOOKING AT ME.
WHY ARE THEY FLAPPING AROUND LIKE A BUNCH OF CHICKENS WITH THEIR HEADS CUT OFF?
WHO KNOWS.
WHO CARES?
DO YOU MIND IF I THROW THESE AWAY?
PLEASE.

THE HARDEST THING ABOUT A PEANUT ALLERGY IS REMEMBERING TO STAY VIGILANT.
ESPECIALLY IF YOU DON'T ACTUALLY HAVE ONE.
IT'S NOT SUCH A BIG DEAL AT HOME . . .
. . . PROVIDED YOU'RE NOT A TOTAL SLACKER ABOUT IT.
BUT EVERYWHERE ELSE, IT'S, LIKE, TERRIFYING HOW EASY IT WOULD BE TO SLIP UP.

CAN I SEE YOUR INHALER?
WHAT?
YOUR ALLERGY THING. LOUANN SAID YOU HAVE THIS INHALER THING YOU CARRY AROUND.
IT'S NOT AN INHALER. IT'S AN INJECTOR.
YEAH, THAT!
IT'S IN MY LOCKER.
FAT LOT OF GOOD IT DOES YOU THERE. IS THAT WHY YOU DIDN'T USE IT IN THE CAFETERIA?
THE REASON I DIDN'T USE IT IN THE CAFETERIA IS I DIDN'T NEED TO.
AND BY THE WAY, NO OFFENSE, BUT IT KIND OF MAKES ME FEEL LIKE A FREAK THAT YOU ASKED ME TO SHOW IT TO YOU.

UM, SADIE? ARE YOU JUST ACTING MAD, OR ARE YOU REALLY MAD?
WELL, HOW WOULD YOU FEEL?
IT'S NOT SOME, I DON'T KNOW, KILLER IPHONE I'M ALL PSYCHED TO BE CARRYING AROUND . . .
. . . OR LEAVING IN MY LOCKER OR WHATEVER.
IF HE EVER FINDS OUT . . .
I DON'T MEAN TO HARSH ON YOU, PERSONALLY.

IT'S JUST . . . IT'S A PIECE OF MEDICAL EQUIPMENT.
NOT A TOY. IT'S PRIVATE. OKAY?
YEAH, SURE . . .
OH, DAVID . . .
I'M SORRY.
SO, UM . . . FRIENDS?
DEFINITELY!
I CAN'T BELIEVE YOU'RE EVEN WILLING TO LOOK AT ME.

BEFORE GYM . . .
WHOO, THIS T-SHIRT IS RANK!
AT LEAST YOU LOOK SEMIHUMAN IN YOURS. I LOOK LIKE . . .
. . . SOMEBODY'S PET ORANGUTAN OR SOMETHING.
WILL YOU STOP PUTTING YOURSELF DOWN?
OH HEY, I ALMOST FORGOT, I MET SOMEONE FROM YOUR OLD SCHOOL!
YOU DID?
LAST WEEKEND WHEN MY COUSIN AND I WENT SKATING.
WHO?
OH SHOOT, I KNEW YOU WERE GONNA ASK THAT. SHANNON? SHARON?
CHERYL?

I THINK SO. YEAH. I'M LIKE 98% SURE.
CURLY HAIR, RIGHT?
DID SHE SAY ANYTHING ABOUT ME?
LIKE WHAT?
I DON'T KNOW. WE USED TO BE REALLY GOOD FRIENDS, BUT SHE GOT ALL WEIRD AFTER SHE CAME BACK FROM CAMP THIS SUMMER.
I MUST'VE CALLED HER A DOZEN TIMES.
YOU KNOW HOW MANY TIMES SHE CALLED ME BACK? ONCE. I WAS LIKE, "WOW, THANKS A LOT."
WHAT A WENCH!
SHE'S PROBABLY JUST JEALOUS CUZ YOUR NEW FRIENDS ARE SO MUCH COOLER.
DO YOU REMEMBER WHO SHE WAS THERE WITH?
SOME DORK. MY COUSIN KNEW HIM. TOTALLY UNMEMORABLE.
SANDY BLOND HAIR?
I DIDN'T NOTICE. HE WAS NOTHING TO SCREAM ABOUT.

NOT LIKE ZOO!
SHUT UP!
MS. SCHMIDT'S GONNA MURDER US. THE BELL RANG LIKE FIVE MINUTES AGO.
WAIT, LOU, YOU DIDN'T TELL CHERYL ANYTHING ABOUT THAT THING WITH THE SQUID CHIP, DID YOU?
WHAT?
IN THE CAFETERIA.
NO, I KNEW WHAT YOU MEANT. IT'S JUST, THAT'D BE KIND OF A RANDOM THING TO BRING UP.
I KNOW, BUT . . .
CHERYL WAS ALWAYS SUPER-FREAKED BY THE PEANUT THING.
EVEN THOUGH WE'RE NOT FRIENDS ANYMORE, AND IT REALLY SUCKS THAT SHE DIDN'T HAVE THE COURTESY TO CALL ME BACK . . .
. . . I WOULDN'T WANT TO WORRY HER.

ALSO, DON'T TAKE THIS THE WRONG WAY, BUT I'D FEEL KIND OF FUNNY IF I FOUND OUT YOU WERE DISCUSSING MEDICAL STUFF BEHIND MY BACK.
YEAH, I KNOW.
DAVID TOLD ME HOW YOU REACTED WHEN HE ASKED TO SEE YOUR ALLERGY PEN.
OKAY, NOW I'M EMBARRASSED.
I THINK I WAS PMS-ING OR SOMETHING. I REALLY WENT OFF ON HIM.
PLEASE! I WOULD'VE DONE THE SAME!
YEAH, BUT HE FELT SO BAD!
YOU'RE BEING WAY TOO SWEET. I'D HAVE TORN HIS HEAD OFF!
I KIND OF DID.
NOT LIKE I WOULD HAVE!

DAVID AND I ARE LIKE THIS. WE DON'T MINCE WORDS.
OKAY, YOU'RE SCARING ME A LITTLE.
IT'S LIKE, DO YOU HAVE ANYONE YOU'RE TOTALLY HONEST WITH?
HE GIVES ME A REASON, HE'S GONNA FEEL THE FULL STRENGTH OF MY WRATH!
UM, SURE.
NO, I MEAN SOMEONE WHO'LL ALWAYS TELL YOU THE TRUTH, NO MATTER HOW GNARLY IT IS. AND YOU DO THE SAME FOR THEM.
WELL, ZOO, I GUESS.
DAVID'S THAT PERSON FOR ME.
I KNOW, YOU GUYS ARE LIKE SIBLINGS, YOU'RE SO TIGHT.
SIBLINGS. RIGHT. YOU WOULDN'T HAPPEN TO BE AN ONLY CHILD, WOULD YOU?
YOU KNOW WHAT I MEAN.
HEY . . .
CAN YOU KEEP A SECRET?

SURE.
I CAN'T BELIEVE I'M TELLING YOU THIS.
WHAT?
DAVID AND I FOOLED AROUND.
WHAT!?
SHHH!
MMMFF!
NOBODY ELSE KNOWS.
WHEN?
WHEN WE WENT PUMPKIN PICKING.
WHAT!!?
WILL YOU HUSH UP YOUR MOUTH?

MMMF MMF MMF.
CAN I TRUST YOU?
MMMF MMF.
WAIT, THOUGH, ZOO AND I WERE WITH YOU GUYS THE WHOLE TIME.
DON'T TELL ME YOU WERE GETTING FREAKY ON THE HAYRIDE!
OF COURSE NOT.
IT WAS AT DAVID'S AFTER ZOO MADE US WATCH THAT DUMB VIDEO. AFTER YOU GUYS LEFT.
BUT YOU LEFT WITH US.
I FORGOT MY PUMPKIN, SO I HAD TO GO BACK.
A LIKELY STORY . . .
I DID!
UH-HUH . . .

C'MON, IT'S NOT LIKE I PLANNED FOR THIS TO HAPPEN.
WHAT DOES DAVID SAY?
NOTHING. HE'S ACTING LIKE IT NEVER HAPPENED.
WHAT HAPPENED TO YOU GUYS BEING COMPLETELY HONEST WITH EACH OTHER?
WE ARE, BUT IT'S WEIRD BECAUSE, YOU KNOW, HE'S MY BEST FRIEND.
SO, IS THIS SOMETHING YOU'D LIKE TO CONTINUE, OR . . . ?
YES!
NO!
I DON'T KNOW!

WAIT, JUST HOW FAR DID YOU GUYS GO?
EXCUSE ME, THAT IS NONE OF YOUR BUSINESS!
YOU CAN'T BRING IT UP AND NOT TELL ME!
FAR ENOUGH, OKAY?
OH MAN, SCHMIDT'S REALLY GOING TO LET US HAVE IT NOW. . . .
FORGET IT. WE'RE TOAST.
WE COULD LIE AND TELL HER WE HAVE OUR PERIODS.
WOULDN'T THAT MAKE, LIKE, FIVE TIMES THIS MONTH?
MIGHT AS WELL GO FOR SIX. MAKE IT A FULL-BLOWN MEDICAL CONDITION.

SO, I'VE GOT A LITTLE CONFESSION TO MAKE, TOO.
OKAY.
I TOTALLY THOUGHT DAVID WAS GAY.
I KNOW! EVERYBODY DOES.
IT'S THE CLOTHES.
WELL, YEAH, BUT ALSO BECAUSE HE'S SO NICE.
DON'T MENTION ANYTHING TO ZOO, OKAY?

I LEFT THE PERMISSION SLIP FOR THAT FIELD TRIP ON YOUR DESK.
HUH?
THE HISTORICAL SOCIETY?
CHOP CHOP
THAT SLIP YOU GAVE ME TO SIGN? HELLO?
OH RIGHT. SORRY, I WAS THINKING ABOUT SOMETHING ELSE.
CLEARLY.
I HEAR THE CURRENT EXHIBIT IS REALLY GOOD.
CHOP
I WAS THINKING MAYBE YOUR FRIEND ZOO COULD JOIN US FOR DINNER THAT NIGHT.
I COULD MAKE MY FAMOUS CHICKEN AND DUMPLINGS.
CHOP
CHOP

EARTH TO SADIE . . .
I DON'T KNOW . . .
IT'S REALLY NICE OF YOU, BUT HE'S SO SHY, I DON'T THINK HE'D BE ALL THAT COMFORTABLE WITH IT.
HE'S NOT SHY WITH YOU, IS HE?
NO, BUT . . .
I JUST DON'T THINK HE'D WANT TO, IS ALL.
ALL RIGHT, WELL . . . MY MISTAKE.
MOM . . .
HEAVEN FORBID THE MARVELOUS ZOO SHOULD BE MADE TO FEEL UNCOMFORTABLE!
CHOP
CHOP
IT'S NOTHING PERSONAL. IT'S JUST HIS SHYNESS.
HE FEELS LIKE HE'S ALWAYS MAKING A BAD IMPRESSION ON PEOPLE.
HE'S CERTAINLY MANAGING TO WITH ME!

YOU DON'T EVEN KNOW HIM!
THANK YOU, I'M QUITE AWARE OF THAT!
CHOP
CHOP
CHOP
IS IT THAT YOU DON'T WANT HIM TO MEET ME?
HE *HAS* MET YOU!
THAT TIME IN FRONT OF THE HOUSE? HE DIDN'T EVEN GET OFF HIS BIKE!
YEAH, WELL, HE'S *SHY*!
AND ALSO, THAT TIME YOU DROPPED ME OFF BEFORE THE SOCCER GAME.
YOU'RE WORRIED I'LL EMBARRASS YOU IF I'M ALLOWED TO TALK TO HIM FOR MORE THAN TWO MINUTES.
THAT IS SO NOT IT.
TOO BAD I'M NOT COOL ENOUGH FOR YOUR NEW FRIENDS.
QUIT.

I'M SORRY, SADIE. IT'S NOT YOU.
YOUR DAD, THE MOVE, SWITCHING SCHOOLS . . . YOU'VE HANDLED ALL THESE CHANGES WITH SO MUCH GRACE.
NOT LIKE ME.
OH, MOM.
IT'LL BE OKAY.
YOU'RE A GREAT KID.
YEAH, RIGHT.
NO, YOU REALLY ARE.
AND WHENEVER YOUR BOYFRIEND FEELS READY, I'D LOVE TO GET TO KNOW HIM BETTER. THAT'S ALL.
OKAY, PUMPKIN?
OKAY.

WHAT IF ONE OF THEM BRINGS UP MY "ALLERGY" IN FRONT OF HER? AND SHE'S ALL LIKE, "WHAT ALLERGY?"

I FELT SICK TO MY STOMACH LIKE FIFTY TIMES A DAY.
ALLOW ME, MADAME.
I THINK THE CLASP MAY BE BROKEN. IT'S NOT SUPPOSED TO FALL OFF LIKE THIS.
ESPECIALLY WHEN I THOUGHT OF HOW I'D PAINTED ZOO AS SOME SORT OF ANTISOCIAL JERK SO MY MOM WOULD BACK OFF.
GOT IT!
MEANWHILE, ZOO HAD PRETTY MUCH DECIDED MY MOM MUST HAVE A PROBLEM WITH ASIAN GUYS.
WHAT!? NO!
YOU'RE SURE THAT'S NOT THE REAL REASON YOU DON'T WANT ME COMING BY YOUR HOUSE?
NO! SHE'S JUST GOT A LOT OF STUFF ON HER PLATE RIGHT NOW.
YOU MEAN LIKE SWEDISH BABY CLOTHES?
NO . . .
LOOK, IS IT OKAY IF WE JUST DROP THE SUBJECT?
WAIT, IT'S NOT MORE MONEY STUFF WITH YOUR DAD, IS IT?
UH-UH.
CARPE DIEM, GIRLIE! WHAT ARE YOU WAITING FOR?
IT'S . . .

NOW OR NEVER! TELL HIM!
FORGET IT. IT'S NOTHING.
IT BORES ME EVEN HAVING TO THINK ABOUT IT.
OKAY, BUT JUST SO YOU KNOW?
I THINK YOU'RE NUTS.
HA HA . . . YEAH.
INTERESTING CHOICE OF WORDS . . .

NOVEMBER

OH!
OH WOW.
IT LOOKS SO REAL.
THAT'S BECAUSE IT IS.
WHAT?
DON'T WORRY. I HAD IT TOTALLY ENCASED IN BRONZE.
THERE'S NO WAY IT CAN HURT YOU.
WHERE DID YOU . . . ?
I ASKED MY MOM WHERE SHE GOT MY BABY SHOES DONE.
THE GUY LOOKED AT ME LIKE I WAS CRAZY, BUT HE DID IT.

DO YOU LIKE IT?
NO—
I LOVE IT!!!
WOW. THAT ZOO IS ONE SUAVE DUDE.
OKAY, NOW YOU HAVE TO GET MARRIED.
SHUT UP!
I'M SERIOUS! YOU GUYS ARE, LIKE, TOO PERFECT TOGETHER!
AND THEN THERE'LL BE ALL THESE CUTE LITTLE SUZUKI-WILDHACKS RUNNING AROUND.
THEY'LL BE LIKE, "AUNTIE LOU! AUNTIE LOU!"

DON'T WORRY. WE WON'T BUST YOUR CHOPS IN FRONT OF ZOO!
ANY DEVELOPMENTS TO REPORT?
WE DECIDED TO KEEP THINGS AS JUST FRIENDS.
FOR NOW OR FOR GOOD?
NOT SURE. IF ANYTHING CHANGES, I'LL LET YOU KNOW.
CHECK IT OUT . . .
IT DOESN'T FREAK YOU OUT?
OF COURSE NOT!
WHEN HE TOLD ME TO CLOSE MY EYES, I WAS LIKE, "IT'S GOING TO BE A PIECE OF CANDY . . .
. . . OR A WORM OR SOMETHING!"

AND THEN I WAS LIKE, "WHOA! THIS FEELS LIKE JEWELRY!"
WOW. DOES THIS MEAN YOU'RE "GOING STEADY"?
OH SURE. JUST LIKE ON *LEAVE IT TO BEAVER.*
OH MY GOSH, THAT IS SO CUTE!
THANKS, MAGGIE.
MY GRANDPARENTS GAVE ME THIS LAST CHRISTMAS.
IT'S REALLY NICE.
I NEVER TAKE IT OFF.
OOH, I WISH THE GUMBALL MACHINE WOULD GIVE ME A TIN CROSS!
WHAT IF YOUR SUPER-HOT BOYFRIEND GAVE YOU A GOLD-PLATED CIRCUS PEANUT INSTEAD?

LADIES, PLEASE! THIS IS ALGEBRA. NOT SOME TATTY GUY DE MAUPASSANT STORY.
IF YOU CANNOT LEAVE OFF ADMIRING EACH OTHER'S BAUBLES, I'M AFRAID THERE WILL HAVE TO BE CONSEQUENCES.
SORRY, MR. LARCH.
SORRY, MR. LARCH.
"SORRY, MR. LARCH."
LOSERS.
AFTER SCHOOL

BRRR. YOU GUYS AREN'T FREEZING?
I AM.
LET'S STOP FOR A HOT CHOCOLATE.
I CAN'T. I PROMISED MY FOLKS I'D BE HOME BY 5.
IT'S ONLY 4:15.
YEAH, BUT I'VE GOT LIKE 4 NOTES TO DROP OFF BEFORE THAT.
YOU'VE GOT TO BE KIDDING.
OH MY GOD, YOU REALLY *ARE* AS STUBBORN AS A MULE!
IT DOESN'T DRIVE YOU INSANE?
HE PUTS UP WITH A LOT ON MY END, TOO.

SPEAKING OF ENDS, I CAN'T FEEL MY BUTT ANYMORE. CAN WE PLEASE GO SOMEWHERE WARM?
YOU COULD COME JUST FOR A TINY BIT.
YES WE'RE OPEN
CRAIG
YEAH, BUT CRAIG LIVES WAY OUT BY THE RESERVOIR.
HE WON'T BE ABLE TO TURN IN HIS REPORT TOMORROW UNLESS I GET THIS TO HIM BY TONIGHT.
DID YOU EVER THINK IT'S MAYBE POSSIBLE TO BE TOO HONORABLE?
HAVE FUN, PEANUT.
OPEN

WHAT ARE YOU MAKING FOR THE BAKE SALE?
WHAT BAKE SALE?
SADIE'S NOT IN CHORUS, YOU AIRHEAD.
OH RIGHT.
CHORUS IS HAVING A BAKE SALE TOMORROW TO HELP PAY FOR OUR NEW OUTFITS.
SUGAR
OOH, THEY'RE SO GORGEOUS!
RED TAFFETA!
EMPIRE WAISTS.
LITTLE BABY SLEEVES.

MEANWHILE, US GUYS ARE STILL STUCK IN SKANKY RENTAL TUXES FROM THE DAWN OF DISCO.
BOOGIE DOWN!
BEG PARDON, MR. SATURDAY NIGHT FEVER, BUT WHAT ARE YOU MAKING?
I'LL BE STOPPING BY DINKY DONUTS ON MY WAY TO SCHOOL.
OH MY GOD, THAT IS SO LAME.
WHAT?
SADIE, TELL HIM.
SO LAME.
YOU SEE?
I'M MAKING LEMON SQUARES. TWO STICKS OF BUTTER, REAL LEMON JUICE . . .
YUM.
WANT TO HELP?
SURE! JUST LET ME CALL MY MOM.
JUST WHAT THE TWO OF YOU NEED—MORE SUGAR.

17
Barbara's Snickerdoodles
HELLO DOLLIES
MELANIE'S SUGAR-FREE ICEBOX LOAF
GRANDMA GRAY'S RASPBERRY STREUSEL SQUARES
CORN MUFFINS
FROM DAVID S.
DINKY DONUTS

SEXY SADIE!
WOW, BUSINESS IS BOOMING.
I KNOW!
OUR LEMON SQUARES SOLD OUT FIRST THING!
LOU, CAN YOU MAKE CHANGE FOR THIS TWENTY?
ANYTHING YOU'D RECOMMEND?
I HOPE YOU'RE NOT PLANNING TO TOUCH FOOD AFTER YOU HANDLE THAT MONEY.
HANDLE THIS, YOU GERMAPHOBIC SOW.
LOU, C'MON! HE'S GOT TO GET TO GYM!
GOD! DOESN'T ANYONE PAY WITH SMALL BILLS ANYMORE?

Peanut Butter Cookies
SOUTHERN STYLE PEANUT FUDGE
CHOCOLATE ZUCCHINI CAKES
WHAT'S THE WORD ON THESE?
ZUCCHINI IN A CUPCAKE? ICK.
DUDE, THOSE ARE AWESOME! THE ZUKE MAKES 'EM CRAZY MOIST.
ARE THEY YOURS?
NO, SOME GIRL'S.
GET 'EM WHILE YOU CAN, CUZ NEXT PERIOD I'M HITTING MY BUDDY UP FOR A TEN SO I CAN COME BACK AND BUY 'EM ALL.

DO YOU KNOW IF THEY HAVE PEANUTS IN THEM?
NAH, NOTHING BUT CHOCOLATY ZUCCHINI GOODNESS.
YOU'RE SURE?
SCOUT'S HONOR.
MIND IF I BUY ONE?
DUDE, IT'S A FREE COUNTRY. JUST DON'T BUY 'EM ALL.
LOUANN, DO YOU HAVE CHANGE FOR A—
I'M LOSING MY *MIND* HERE!
WHATEVER YOU WANT, JUST TAKE IT, OKAY? PAY ME AT LUNCH!
ONE FOR ZOO, TOO, OKAY?
WHATEVER!

L-DOG!
TACO-BELLITA!
LOOK AT YOU, ALL SCHOOL-SPIRITED AND STUFF.
WHEN'D YOU TURN INTO SUCH A GOODY-GOODY?
I CUT CHORUS SO MUCH, MS. DEMMING'S GOING TO KICK ME OUT IF I CAN'T DEMONSTRATE THAT I CARE.

DO YOU?
DUH! OF COURSE!
DO YOU EVEN KNOW WHERE WE STAY IF WE MAKE IT TO STATE FINALS? THE GRAND HYATT.
OOH, PARTY.
DID I FORGET TO MENTION THAT PAUL C IS A TENOR?
MEANING HE, TOO, WILL BE STAYING AT THE GRAND HYATT?
YOU HOOKER. GIMME SOME OF THOSE ROUND THINGS.
NOT NOW.

CHOCOLATE ZUCCHINI CAKES. SOUNDS COMPARATIVELY HEALTHY.
NO CHANGE NECESSARY, MS. AVERY.
THANKS, MR. LARCH.
AH, MS. WILDHACK . . .
SUPPORTING THE CHORUS?
MMPHF. 'OU TOO?
MM. DELISSHUSSH.

TELL ME YOU'RE NOT EATING THE SAME THING I AM!
IT'S A CHOCOLATE ZUCCHINI—

GET THE NURSE! TELL HER WE HAVE AN EMERGENCY!
MR. LARCH—
RUN!
SOMEONE CALL 911!
WHERE'S YOUR PURSE?
WHAT?
OH NO, IT'S SADIE.

YOUR PEN! WE NEED YOUR PEN!
I . . . UH, I DON'T—
SHIT! ANGELA, WHAT'D YOU DO WITH MY PURSE? IT'S GOT MY PHONE!
I PUT IT IN MY LOCKER LIKE YOU SAID!
NO ONE PANIC!
I DON'T SEE IT!!! YOU HAVE TO SHOW ME!
UM—
SHE'S DISORIENTED!

WAIT!
LOVE
ZOO

OH GOD!
OH GOD!
I NEED TO REPORT AN EMERGENCY AT PCHS.
YES, HELLO? I'M CALLING ABOUT A GIRL AT PLAINFIELD HIGH—SOMETHING'S REALLY WRONG WITH HER!
I THINK SHE MAY BE DIABETIC!
BY THE TROPHY CASES!
A TEACHER'S GOT HER DOWN ON THE FLOOR!
. . . PCHS . . .
. . . EMERGENCY
. . . GIRL . . .

OH GOD, WHERE'S ZOO?
WHAT'S HIS NUMBER?
TELL THEM SHE'S ALLERGIC TO PEANUTS!
STAY WITH US, SADIE!!!
WAIT, MR. LARCH—
DON'T TRY TO TALK! STAY CALM! TAKE DEEP BREATHS!
OKAY.
HOWARD! WHAT'S GOING ON?
MAKE WAY! GIVE 'EM ROOM!

OH GOD, I THINK SHE'S THE ONE WHO'S ALLERGIC TO PEANUTS!
{GASP!} YOU'RE RIGHT!
SEE HER NECKLACE? MARCY SAYS IT'S PART OF A SUICIDE PACT SHE HAS WITH HER BOYFRIEND!
NO!
SHE WAS EATING ONE OF THESE WHEN I FOUND HER.
FOR REAL, YOU CRACK IT OPEN, AND THERE'S AN ACTUAL PEANUT.
SADIE? HOW ARE YOU FEELING?
I SEARCHED HER BAG! THAT PEN THING IS NOWHERE TO BE FOUND!
ARE YOU HAVING TROUBLE BREATHING?
I DON'T THINK SO.
CAN YOU TELL ME WHAT IT WAS THAT YOU ATE?
UH, MY REGULAR BREAKFAST AND THEN TWO CHOCOLATE ZU—
I HAD THE SAME AND IMMEDIATELY DETECTED A NUT!
NOT A WHOLE ONE, BUT—

OKAY, SADIE, HAVE YOU GOT YOUR EPIPEN ON YOU?
IT'S . . .
IT'S . . .
I THINK I MIGHT'VE LEFT IT AT HOME.
GODDAMMIT!!!
HOWARD, TAKE A BREATH.
I'VE GOT EMERGENCY SUPPLIES OF EPINEPHRINE IN MY CABINET.
LET'S GET HER UP!
ARE YOU GOOD TO WALK?

I HEAR SIRENS!
OH THANK GOD!
SOMEBODY MEET THEM AT THE MAIN DOOR! LEAD THEM IN!
ON IT!
ARE WE STILL GOING TO YOUR OFFICE?
THE PARAMEDICS WILL BE HERE ANY SEC, HON. LET'S JUST SIT TIGHT.
PLEASE?
PLEASE CAN WE GO TO YOUR OFFICE?

OKAY, LET'S GO.
KEVIN, WHEN THE PARAMEDICS SHOW UP, YOU SEND THEM TO MY OFFICE.
OKAY.
I'LL NOTIFY HER PARENTS!
THAT'S AN EXCELLENT IDEA.
WAIT—

OH MY GOD!
I HOPE SHE'S OKAY!
I WAS LIKE, "OH MY GOD, IS SHE CHOKING?"
WHAT DID SHE EAT?
A PEANUT BUTTER COOKIE!
DEATH BY BAKE SALE!
LARCH WAS TOTALLY FREAKING OUT!
"GODDAMMIT!!!"
"NOBODY PANIC!!!"
WHO MADE THE THING WITH PEANUTS?
WHOEVER DID, I BET THEY'RE FEELING PRETTY GUILTY!
MY UNCLE'S GOT THE EXACT SAME THING, EXCEPT HE'S ALLERGIC TO STRAWBERRIES.
{???}
WHAT'S GOING ON?
DAVID, OH GOD, YOU TOTALLY MISSED IT.
SADIE ATE A PEANUT.
WHY ARE ALL THOSE FLASHING RED LIGHTS OUT FRONT?

911
FCHS

EPILOGUE

SOMETIMES I WISH I COULD GO BACK TO MY OLD SCHOOL . . .

. . . THE ONE WHERE NO ONE KNEW ABOUT MY "PEANUT ALLERGY."

THOUGH, THANKS TO THE MIRACLE OF MODERN COMMUNICATION . . .

. . . THEY PROBABLY DO NOW.

NEXT TIME YOU'RE TEMPTED TO BEND THE TRUTH . . .
. . . TAKE MY ADVICE AND DON'T.

SOONER OR LATER IT'LL ALL COME OUT . . .
AND THEN YOU'LL WISH YOU REALLY HAD GONE INTO ANAPHYLACTIC SHOCK . . . AND DIED.
FD
FALSE ALARM, FELLAS.

THOSE 911 GUYS REALLY LOVE FINDING OUT THAT THEIR TIME'S BEEN WASTED. I GUESS THEY MADE SOME COMMENTS ON THE WAY OUT.
I'VE HEARD OF FAKING AN ORGASM, BUT A PEANUT ALLERGY?
GIRLS, DO US A FAVOR. NEXT TIME YOU'RE HAVING A BAKE SALE, LOSE THE NUTS.
SHE'S NUTS, ALL RIGHT.
HEY, FRANK, NEXT TIME THIS JOINT'S UP FOR INSPECTION, GIVE 'EM A CITATION FOR FAILING TO CHARGE THEIR POLYGRAPH!
HAR HAR!!!
911

MY MOM WASN'T TOO PLEASED WITH ME, EITHER.

THE FACT THAT YOU WENT TO SUCH EXTREMES . . .
ORDERING A MEDICAL BRACELET OFF THE INTERNET!
PUTTING IT ON EVERY TIME YOU LEFT THE HOUSE.
HIDING IT BEFORE COMING BACK IN.
LYING TO YOUR TEACHERS.
THE NURSE.
ME.
I BARELY KNOW WHERE TO START.

YOU'RE SURE NONE OF YOUR NEW FRIENDS PUT YOU UP TO THIS?
IN A PERFECT WORLD, EVERYONE WOULD BE AS WILLING TO FORGIVE AS MY MOM TURNED OUT TO BE. . . .

LOUANN WAS LIKE . . . I'VE NEVER SEEN ANYONE THAT FURIOUS.
I MEAN, NOT THAT SHE DOESN'T HAVE EVERY RIGHT TO BE. . . .

IT'S KIND OF HARD FOR ME TO EVEN THINK ABOUT IT.
DAVID? I DON'T KNOW. MAYBE WE'D STILL BE FRIENDS, IF IT WEREN'T FOR LOUANN. . . . MAYBE NOT.
ANGELA DROPPED ME, TOO, BUT IT'S NOT LIKE THE TWO OF US WERE ALL THAT CLOSE TO BEGIN WITH.
PCHS
PLAINFIELD COMMUNITY HIGH SCHOOL

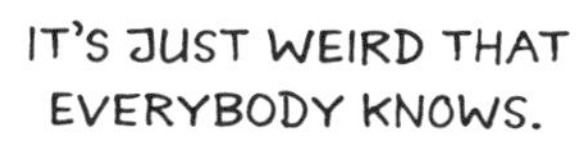
IT'S JUST WEIRD THAT
EVERYBODY KNOWS.

LOTS OF THEM DON'T ACTUALLY KNOW
ME, THEY JUST KNOW ABOUT "IT."

I'M FAMOUS . . .
. . . IN THE GROSSEST, MOST
HUMILIATING, SELF-INFLICTED
SORT OF WAY.

PEOPLE GO OUT OF THEIR
WAY TO IGNORE ME.

WELL DONE,
MS. PETERSON!

I'D SUGGEST WORKING IN PENCIL, MR. MENDOZA. THEY HAVE ERASERS.
I GUESS I'M NOT THE ONLY ONE WHO FEELS LIKE THE WHOLE WORLD IS LAUGHING AT ME.
IN MY CASE, I HAVE NO ONE BUT MYSELF TO BLAME.
TEMPTING AS IT MAY BE . . .
I'M EXTREMELY ALLERGIC TO PEANUTS!
ONE LITTLE TASTE AND I'M DEAD!
OH GOD, DOES THIS YOGURT HAVE PEANUTS IN IT!!?!
NOOOOO!

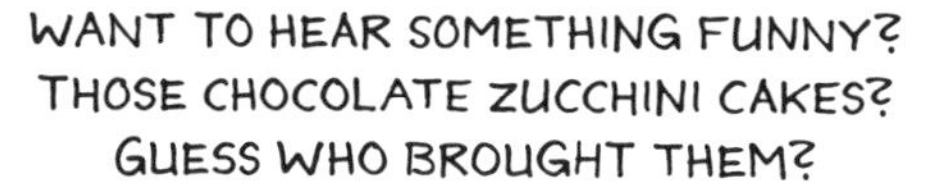

I HEARD HER MOM'S EARTHY-CRUNCHY TO THE NTH POWER. ERGO THE ZUCCHINI.

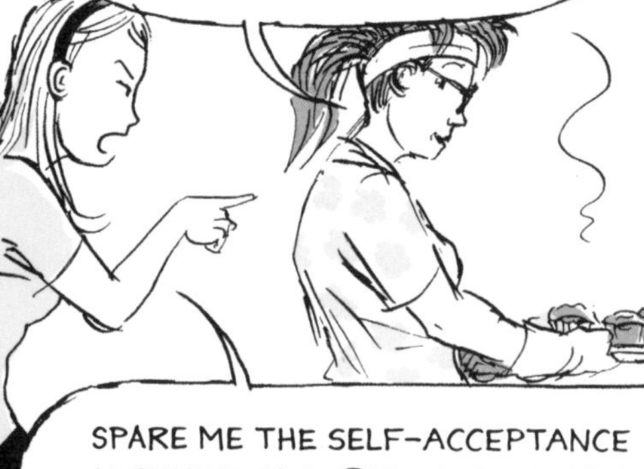

WANT TO HEAR SOMETHING ELSE?

THOSE CAKES DIDN'T *HAVE* PEANUTS.

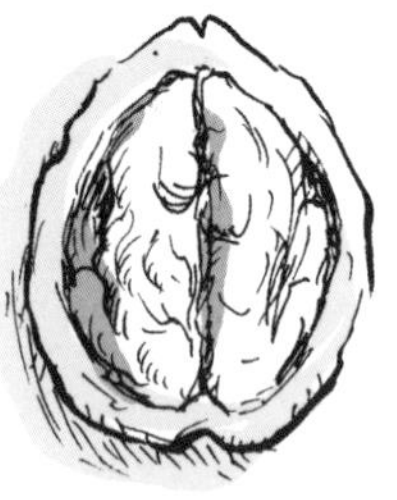

NOT ONE.

YOU'D THINK SOMEONE AS SMART AS MR. LARCH COULD DISTINGUISH BETWEEN A PEANUT AND A WALNUT. . . .

I GUESS THERE'S A REASON HE DOESN'T TEACH BIOLOGY. . . .
THE MAN'S AS NUTTY AS A FRUITCAKE!

JRSE

OH MY GAWWD, IT'S THE MISSING HEALTH FORM.

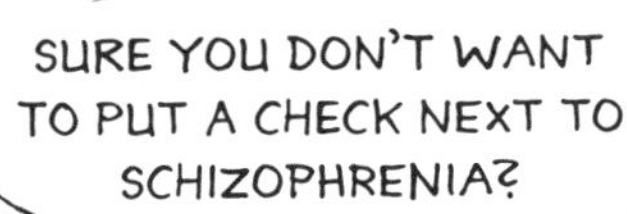
SURE YOU DON'T WANT TO PUT A CHECK NEXT TO SCHIZOPHRENIA?

I'M KIDDING! BUT YOU'VE GOT TO ADMIT THAT I DESERVE A LITTLE FUN . . .
. . . AFTER WHAT YOU PUT ME THROUGH!

ONE OF THESE DAYS, THE MEN IN WHITE COATS ARE GOING TO COME CART ME OFF TO THE LOONY BIN.
AWW, YOU KNOW I'M HERE FOR ALL MY KIDS.
IT DOESN'T HAVE TO BE SOME BIG EMERGENCY. IN FACT, I PREFER IT WHEN IT'S NOT!
COME BY WHENEVER YOU'RE IN THE MOOD FOR A CHAT. HOW'S THAT?
I'D LIKE THAT.
CHIN UP, KIDDO!

AND THEN THERE WAS ZOO.
YOU HATE ME.

HATE'S A PRETTY STRONG WORD.
MOMMY DOESN'T LIKE FOR ME TO USE IT.
SO MUCH FOR DEFLATING TENSION WITH HUMOR.
YOU DON'T HAVE TO BE FUNNY FOR MY SAKE.
ALL RIGHT. THANKS, I GUESS.
THE WHOLE THING'S PRETTY HUMILIATING, HUH?

I JUST WISH YOU'D TRUSTED ME MORE.
OH, ZOO, I DID. I DO. . . .
I SHOULD GIVE THIS BACK.
KEEP IT.
I'M SURE IF I THOUGHT ABOUT IT, I COULD COME UP WITH 50 MILLION USES FOR A BRONZED PEANUT, BUT . . .
I DON'T THINK I'LL BE WEARING IT MUCH.
NO OFFENSE.
NONE TAKEN.

ACTUALLY, I WILL TAKE IT BACK, IF YOU DON'T MIND.
IT WAS KIND OF EXPENSIVE.
I UNDERSTAND. HERE.
OKAY, THANKS.
I GUESS I'M GOING TO GO NOW.
THERE'S SOMETHING I HAVE TO DO.
OKAY.
I'LL SEE YOU AROUND.
YEAH. BYE.

MAYBE IF I HAD IT TO DO OVER AGAIN, I COULD TRY A DIFFERENT ANGLE. PEOPLE MAKE FRIENDS ANY NUMBER OF WAYS, RIGHT?
I COULD JOIN THE VOLLEYBALL TEAM . . .
. . . OR THE SCHOOL PAPER OR THE HOMECOMING COMMITTEE . . .
PCHS NEWS
SADIE'S STORY
PCHS DRAMA GROUP PRESENTS
OKLAHOMA!
AUDITIONS
THIS FRIDAY
. . . OR TRY OUT FOR THE FALL MUSICAL . . .
. . . OR START A PETITION TO GET A SODA MACHINE IN THE CAFETERIA . . .
Cola
. . . OR HANG OUT WITH THE STONER KIDS. SO WHAT IF I DON'T SMOKE POT?
DUDE, THAT IS MESSED UP!

NO POSING AS A PERUVIAN EXCHANGE STUDENT.
NO INVENTING A CONDITION I DON'T HAVE.
BULIMIC
BIPOLAR
ADD
ASPERGER'S SYNDROME
OBSESSIVE-COMPULSIVE
ALCOHOLIC
DIABETIC
EPILEPTIC
LIAR

THAT NIGHT
DEE-DELEE!
HELLO?
SADIE!!! PHONE!!!
WHO IS IT?
HE DIDN'T SAY . . .
SOME BOY!!!

BLOW!
HELLO?
I NEED YOUR NUMBER.
. . . ZOO?
I'VE GOT THE AREA CODE. WHAT COMES AFTER?
IT'S . . .
YOU JUST CALLED IT.

NOT YOUR HOME PHONE, DING-DONG. YOUR CELL PHONE!
OH. IT'S 3-0-4-
5-9.
WAIT. 6 . . . 9
MAGICAL MYSTERY TOUR
WHAT?
5-9. NOT 6-9.

ARRGH!
HOW DO YOU GET THIS STUPID THING TO GO BACK?
IS THERE A CLEAR BUTTON?
WHAT?
LOOK FOR A BUTTON THAT SAYS "C."
THIS IS RIDICULOUS.
LET'S GO BACK TO THE BEGINNING.
GOOD IDEA.
OKAY. 3-0-4 . . .
5-9-6 . . .

NEXT MORNING
SO, YEAH, THERE'S NO CHANGING THE PAST . . .
AND FORGET ABOUT CONTROLLING THE FUTURE.
ALL THAT'S LEFT IS TO LIVE IN THE PRESENT, WHATEVER THAT MEANS.

No matter how much it sucks,
I'm glad your emergency wasn't real.
Next time you get into a jam,
call me, okay ?!!?
Love, Zoe
P.S.-Giving out my number is punishable by death! For emergency use only!
P.P.S.-Please be patient while I figure out how to use this stupid thing.
I KNOW IT'S CORNY, BUT
I ♥ YOU JUST THE WAY YOU ARE
BLEEB
BLEEB
TWEEDLE-EE-DEEDLE-EE-DEEDLE-EE-DEE
?

TWEEDLE-EE-DEEDLE-EE-DEE!
!
TWEEDLE-EE-DEEDLE-EE-DEE
AIIIEEEE!!!
CRASH!
TWEEDLE-EE-
SADIE!

I DON'T BELIEVE IT! YOU PICKED UP!
WHAT'S GOING ON?

THE END

PUBLISHED IN THE UNITED STATES BY SCHWARTZ & WADE BOOKS, AN IMPRINT OF RANDOM HOUSE CHILDREN'S BOOKS, A DIVISION OF RANDOM HOUSE, INC., NEW YORK.

SCHWARTZ & WADE BOOKS AND THE COLOPHON ARE TRADEMARKS OF RANDOM HOUSE, INC.

VISIT US ON THE WEB! RANDOMHOUSE.COM/TEENS

EDUCATORS AND LIBRARIANS, FOR A VARIETY OF TEACHING TOOLS, VISIT US AT
RHTEACHERSLIBRARIANS.COM

LIBRARY OF CONGRESS CATALOGING-IN-PUBLICATION DATA
HALLIDAY, AYUN.
PEANUT / AYUN HALLIDAY ; ILLUSTRATED BY PAUL HOPPE.—1ST ED.
P. CM.
SUMMARY: NERVOUS ABOUT STARTING HER SOPHOMORE YEAR AT A NEW HIGH SCHOOL, SADIE DECIDES TO MAKE HERSELF MORE INTERESTING BY CLAIMING TO BE ALLERGIC TO PEANUTS, BUT HER LIE QUICKLY SPIRALS OUT OF CONTROL.
ISBN 978-0-375-86590-9 (TRADE) — ISBN 978-0-375-96590-6 (GLB)
978-0-307-97909-4 (EBOOK)
1. GRAPHIC NOVELS. [1. GRAPHIC NOVELS. 2. FOOD ALLERGY—FICTION. 3. POPULARITY—FICTION. 4. HIGH SCHOOLS—FICTION. 5. SCHOOLS—FICTION. 6. MOVING, HOUSEHOLD—FICTION. 7. MOTHERS AND DAUGHTERS—FICTION.] I. HOPPE, PAUL, ILL. II. TITLE.
PZ7.7.H36PE 2011
[FIC]—DC22
2009047168

THE TEXT OF THIS BOOK IS SET IN HOPPE.
THE ILLUSTRATIONS WERE DRAWN BY HAND USING PEN AND INK AND COLORED DIGITALLY.
BOOK DESIGN BY RACHAEL COLE

MANUFACTURED IN SINGAPORE

10 9 8 7 6 5 4 3 2 1

FIRST EDITION

RANDOM HOUSE CHILDREN'S BOOKS SUPPORTS THE FIRST AMENDMENT
AND CELEBRATES THE RIGHT TO READ.

AYUN HALLIDAY writes and illustrates *The East Village Inky,* a long-running, award-winning autobiographical zine. She is also the author of the picture book *Always Lots of Heinies at the Zoo,* four memoirs, and a guidebook to New York City. Ms. Halliday lives in Brooklyn, New York, with her husband and two children. Visit her at ayunhalliday.com.

PAUL HOPPE's illustrations have appeared in many publications, including the *New York Times,* the *Wall Street Journal,* and the *New Yorker*. He is the cofounder and art director of the comic anthology *Rabid Rabbit*. He has published two graphic novels in Germany and two picture books for children, *Hat* and *The Woods*. Born in Poland and raised in Germany, Mr. Hoppe now lives and works in Brooklyn, New York. Learn more at paulhoppe.com.